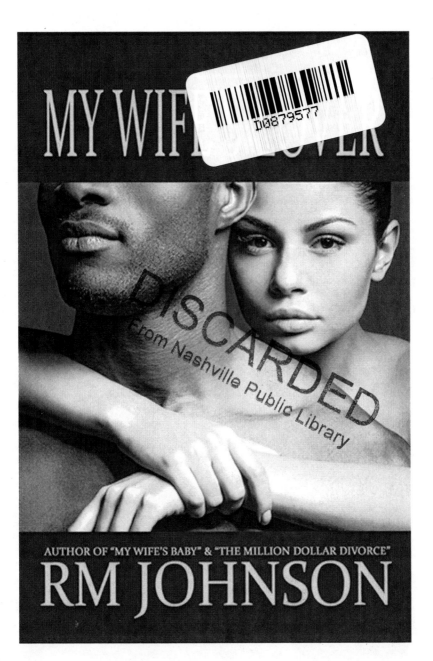

MY WIFE'S LOVER

AUTHOR OF "MY WIFE'S BABY" & "THE MILLION DOLLAR DIVORCE"

RM JOHNSON

2

MY WIFE'S LOVER

A Novel

RM JOHNSON

Published by MarcusArts, LLC

This is a work of fiction. Names, characters, businesses, places, events and incidents are either the produces of the author's imagination or used in a fictitious manner. Any resemblance to actual persons, living or dead, or actual events is purely coincidental.

Also by RM Johnson

Hate the Air: The Abbreviated Life of Shea Kennedy
My Wife's Baby
Bishop 3
Bishop 2
Bishop
Keeping the Secret 3
Keeping the Secret 2
Keeping the Secret
Deceit and Devotion
No One in the World with E. Lynn Harris
Why Men Fear Marriage
Stacie and Cole
The Million Dollar Demise
The Million Dollar Deception
The Million Dollar Divorce
Do You Take This Woman
Dating Games
Love Frustration
Father Found
The Harris Family
The Harris Men

MY WIFE'S LOVER

A Novel

RM JOHNSON

Marcusarts LLC—Atlanta, GA

1

I watched my wife park in front of the large brick house with burgundy awnings. She climbed out her car and took the stairs up. From behind the wheel of my SUV, I witnessed the front door open, a bare-chested man reach out, take my wife's hand, pull her into him and as his smiling face hung over her shoulder, one of his hands grabbed her ass, causing her to throw back her head and laugh. He pulled her into the house then stuck his head out, looking up and down the street for anyone who might've observed what he was doing.

I ducked quickly behind the dash of my truck, feeling foolish, cowardly, afraid to be seen by the man fucking the woman I thought was my soul mate.

I sat frozen by indecision, staring up at the house, wondering what was happening that moment. Why wonder when I knew, when I could see it in my head: the man leading my wife up the stairs, or was she was in front, him watching as she climbed up, her bare ass jumping under the sheer dress she had purchased for him, his dick growing hard inside his silk pajama bottoms.

I shut my eyes, banged a fist on the dash. "Go in there, Stan! Goddamn it!"
I said, knowing what would take place in there if I didn't: the teasing: lips pressed together in the exchange of saliva, breasts groped, testicles

fondled. Then what would happen after that: Michael's head buried between my wife's thighs, his dick ending up in her mouth, then him bending her over, rolling up behind her, slapping her ass. I knew I could not afford to sit.

I snatched the key from the ignition, threw the truck door open, ran across Michael's front lawn, up the stairs. At the door, I started to ring the doorbell, but didn't. Trying the knob, it turned. Inside, clothes were strewn across the living room floor: my wife's dress, her thong, her shoes, her bra.

I hurried down the second floor hallway, praying what I feared was happening, wasn't. I stopped at the open bedroom door. Inside my wife lay naked on her belly, her head hanging off one side of the bed. Michael stood just as naked in front of her, his back to me, my wife grabbing him between the legs. I couldn't see what she was doing, but heard the loud slurping sounds of her lips lubricated by her spit as her mouth slid back and forth over the man enlarged penis.

Tears stinging my eyes, I watched the man's legs tremble, his fists in my wife's hair, pulling her into him. I heard him demand she suck him harder. She did then eased away, used her hand, stroked him up and down. "I want you to come like this," I heard her say.

He pleaded with her, his back arching, telling her no.

She laughed, giggled sensually, like she never had with me. Insisting that was what she wanted: his come in her mouth, on her lips, in her hair, on her face. The two were totally wrapped up in this evilness, so consumed they didn't see me there.

He playfully pushed her hands away, leaned back, his dick shiny-wet with her juices. He grabbed her by an arm, threw her around on the bed like a doll. She let herself be tossed, hiking her ass up, spreading her knees open on the mattress.

"Don't do it," I mumbled to myself, walking right up on the doorway, but unable to walk in. "Don't!"

He spread my wife's cheeks, dropped to his knees, stuck his tongue between her thighs, slurping loudly, causing her to cry hysterically and at the same time try to squirm away from him. He held her tight, continued, until she was crying, begging, "Give me that dick! Please, Michael! Fuck me with that dick!"

He stood, but before taking my wife, he looked over his shoulder as if knowing I was there, as if he had left the front door open downstairs for me to come in and see this.

I stared, shocked at him, him smiling back at me, slowly pushing into my wife, her entire body shaking on the bed, her face buried into a pillow, her muffled cries of pleasure sounding more to me like she was being murdered. I couldn't take it. It had to stop it.

As if not worried about me retaliating, he turned his head from me, laying both his hands on my wife, thrusting his hips into her behind, the sound of slapping wet flesh filling the room.

I'd seen enough. I pulled the gun from out my pocket, walked over the bedroom threshold, stood behind him, pressed the tip of the pistol to his head as sweat poured over his shoulders, down his back, into the crack of his ass. This was nothing I wanted to do. But I would never be rid of him any other way. My fist trembling around the gun, my arm aching, I pulled back on the trigger and—

I snapped out of my thoughts to see the back of my wife's head. She was lying in bed, her back to me: the way she had been sleeping for the past three months, when before we always faced each other, always said goodnight and kissed before falling off to sleep.

"Erica," I whispered. She lay unmoving in front of me, pretending to be sleep. But I knew her breathing, exactly how it sounded when she was sleeping badly, peacefully, or not at all: just pretending. Which was what she was doing that moment.

A hand on her shoulder, I gently shook her. "Erica."

"What Stan?" She said over her shoulder, her voice groggy.

"We need to talk about what happened today."

She sighed heavily. Still not turning to me, she said, "We already talked about it. Why go there again?"

What Erica was referring to was when I came home early from work, walked into my house and finding my wife standing in the middle of the living room with another man, her arms around him, as he clutched her around the waist, his head on her shoulder.

"What? What is he doing here?" I said, moving toward them then, contemplating whether to toss the man out by his collar, or first, beat the living shit out of him. I stopped abruptly when my wife's eyes hit mine. One arm around Michael's back, she held up the finger of the other hand, signaling for me to stop. The look she gave me said I could no way understand what was happening, that it was a life and death matter and if I'd just give her a moment to handle it everything would be explained.

But that wasn't enough for me. Fists clenched, chest heaving at the sight of my wife embracing not just another man in my living room, but the same fucking man she cheated on me with three years ago, I demanded an explanation. "Tell me what's going on, Erica. Right now!"

Michael didn't lift his face from my wife's shoulder, just allowed her to deal with me.

"Please, just go into the kitchen or something, Stan. Let me handle this. I promise I'll explain everything," she said, her hand on the nape of the sobbing man's neck, the tips of her fingers soothingly caressing the fine hairs back there.

I was fuming, but for some reason I trusted her, and after telling her: "This better be as important as you're saying it is," I went to the kitchen and waited behind the closed door.

"It's been a long day. Can't this wait?" Erica said, the both of us in bed now, her making no effort to roll over and face me.

"Please," I asked.

Fighting with the comforter, tossing the pillow across the bed, she turned to face me. "What's wrong, Stan?"

"We…" My voice sounded incredibly loud in the dark quiet of our bedroom. I lowered it and started again. "We can do counseling, Erica. Pope said he knows a good—"

"I don't care who Pope knows. There's no need for us to go to therapy. Her tone was conversational, but there was anger in it also.

"So you think we're okay?"

"We're fine, Stan. Go to sleep. I don't want you to be tired at work tomorrow."

"There are things we need to discuss."

"Like what?"

"I want to talk about Michael, the father of your child."

"You're the father of my child," Erica said, crossing her arms over the comforter.

"That's what we agreed to," I said. "But considering he went against the contract he signed, broke the promise he made by showing up here, I don't know anymore."

"You don't know what anymore, Stan?"

"You have that tone with me why?" I said, fed up. "Exactly what am I doing wrong other than trying to save our marriage? Is there a reason why you're snapping my head off just because I want to talk to you?"

Erica sighed, loosened the fold of her arms across her chest then turned to me. "You're right. I'm sorry. What do you want to know?"

"I want to know why he was here?"

"You know why he was here," she snapped then apologized.

"Do I have to be worried?"

"About what?"

"Have you been seeing him?"

"No!" She answered immediately.

"Do you intend to?"

Pause. "No."

"Do you remember that day you had Michael in this house, the day you told me that David might be his."

"How can I forget?"

"You didn't have to do that. You didn't have to tell the truth, but you did, because you've always said you were honest, and have always proven to be. I could've walked away that day, but you promised me we'd raise David as our son, that I'd be his father, and that he would never be taken away from me."

Her head on her pillow, she nodded in agreement, but said nothing.

"So I believed you, as I still do, and I've allowed myself to love that boy. I've invested totally in him, in all that we have here. The two of you are what's most important in this world to me. I'll do anything to hang onto you. I'd kill for the two of you."

"Don't be ridiculous. No one's asking you to kill for—"

"But I would," I said nearing her, my eyes widened with the intensity of my conviction. That's how much you mean to me. Do you understand?"

"I understand," she said, looking a little freaked out.

"Promise me you'll never take David away. That you'll never give him back to Michael."

"Stan, he signed a contract, and—"

"I don't care what he signed. That's not what I'm asking you. Will you promise me, if somehow it becomes possible, that you'll never give David back to him."

Erica sat up in bed, leaned close to me, and with our noses not an inch apart, she stared me in the eyes and said, "I promise." She kissed me softly on the lips. Eyes open, my lips pressed to hers, I watched her as though I wasn't sure if I could trust her words.

"Go to bed," Erica said. "I'll make you eggs in the morning." She rolled over on her side, her back to me, and went to sleep.

I sat up, the blankets falling to the waist of my bare torso, unable to shake the jarring feeling of abandonment, waking to find myself alone in bed. That had been a new thing: Erica getting up without waking me, when before she'd snuggle next to me, stir me awake by kissing me softly on the cheek, or by playing, childlike, with my ears or nose, or sometimes slipping under the comforter, taking me in her mouth until I released. Now every morning, she was invariably absent as though her duty was to sleep in the same bed with me, but wanting to spend as little time as possible there.

Fully dressed: shirt, tie, jeans and loafers, I walked into the kitchen.

"Hi, Dawdy!" My chubby-cheeked son, David said from his high chair. His sandy colored hair growing longer each day, the boy was beautiful: bright eyed, his skin the color of the Cheerios that lay scattered about his highchair tray. He smiled, reaching out two little hands covered in some kind of gooey, warm breakfast cereal. He wore a bib, spattered with the stuff that was on his fingers.

"How's my little man?" I said as excited as he was. I pulled a wet-nap from the dispenser on the table, quickly cleaned his hands, then

16

hoisted him out of the seat onto my hip, while swiping a few of the loose Cheerios and popping them into my mouth.

"It smells good," I said to my beautiful wife, Erica: fair skinned, slender/shapely and big-eyed; she had grown her hair from the cropped style she used to wear when we first met. She stood at the stove scrambling the eggs she had promised me. I leaned over her back, kissed her cheek.

She smiled, and told me to take a seat. "Breakfast will be ready in a minute."

We sat eating in relative quiet: Erica sipping from her coffee, me enjoying the eggs and sausage, David making enough noise so the little conversation that was had between me and my wife didn't feel totally awkward.

"We okay about our conversation last night?" Erica asked, peaking at me over the rim of her coffee mug.

I was in mid sip from my mug. I set my cup down, finished swallowing. "Yeah. But there's more to talk about. We'll be able talk again, right?"

Her expression was mildly pained, but she smiled through it. "Yeah, sure."

"Good." I wiped my mouth with a napkin and stood. "I need to be getting to class and drop this little guy off," I said turning to David, preparing to pull him from his high chair when Erica stopped me.

"You going to get knew tires for the Volvo aren't you?"

The tread on my tires were running a little low, not dangerously low, but low enough for Erica to be concerned after one of her girlfriends spun out on a slippery highway and almost killed herself and her two toddlers. Difference being, her girlfriend's tires were bald as her toddler's heads. I still had about a month of tread left on mine before needing to replace them.

"Yeah. I told you I'll order them next week. I think the price might go down."

"The price?" Erica said, picking up her coffee mug. "Well maybe you don't need to be taking David to daycare until next week then."

"The tires are safe," I said.

"I don't think they are."

"You think I'd believe they were unsafe and still allow our son to ride with me?"

Taking a sip, she said, "I don't know."

"You don't know?"

Her nose buried in her mug, she managed to say: "I don't."

"Is this you trying to drag me into another fight? If so, I'm not doing it, Erica. Not this morning."

"I'm not dragging you into anything," she said standing, grabbing her plate and mine, walking them over, setting them in the sink and turning on the faucet. "I told you about those tires last month, and you still haven't gotten them. I can't chance anything happening to my baby."

"Your baby?" I said, as though I was surprised at her calling David that, even though lately, she's been referring to him more as hers than ours.

"You know what I mean," she said, turning her back on me, grabbing the bottle of dish soap, squirting some on the dishes.

I knew this was one more example of her questioning whether or not I should be trusted with our son, one more opportunity to argue with me.

"Fine," I relented. "I'll get the tires after work today," I said, speaking to my wife's back. "But is this about more than the tires on my truck? I know it is?"

Erica faced me, dishwater suds climbing up her forearms. "No, Stan. This is just about the safety of our son."

2

I sat in the parking lot, the truck still running as I stared out at mothers and fathers carrying their children up to the door of the daycare center. I wondered if any of them were dealing with what I was going through: if either one of them might've been on the verge of losing their son or daughter.

It happened to me during my first marriage. I was young, had lost my job, spent years out of work, all to the dissatisfaction of my first wife, Serena. She thought I hadn't tried hard enough to find work, labeled me lazy, told herself I cared little for our daughter, Janis, or I would've found employment. Serena wanted a divorce, threatened to take custody of our little girl when she was seven years old. I wouldn't allow it, so Serena gathered paperwork, started making the case for why I was unfit: years I spent out of work, the drinking problem I had back then that persists a bit to this day. Her case became more convincing everyday, so I did what had to be done to prevent me from losing my little girl. I packed my daughter's things and a few of my own, threw it all in a bag and we took off: drove to Florida, no plan in mind but to keep my daughter by my side. Unfortunately, my money ran out after only a month, and we had no choice but return. At home, Serena threatened to press charges, have me thrown in jail for kidnapping if I didn't sign away all of my custodial rights. I had no choice. Serena had stolen Janis away from me for a decade: a mistake my ex-wife owns up now to making: a mistake that might be the explanation for why my daughter's life was now falling apart. But that's another story.

Erica said I had no reason to be concerned about losing David as I had lost Janis, but David was hers. I glanced up at the rearview mirror, saw the boy smiling up at me from the backseat.

My wife, Erica, never knew I had a vasectomy a dozen years ago, for I had never told her, so even if I wanted to have played a part in conceiving David, I could not have.

David belonged to another man: the married man my wife had been sleeping with for the ten years prior to meeting me. She had told me about him on our third or fourth date, said that she had ended it because he wouldn't leave his wife for Erica, as he had promised.

But a night came when she excitedly told me she was pregnant. I told her I was happy for her—for us, telling myself I'd wait to confirm there was no way it could be mine before I busted her out, and walked out of her life. But walking in the door with the medical test results saying that there was no way I was able to have fathered the baby she was pregnant with, I saw Erica in our living room with a man: the father.

She brought him there to tell him that he might've been the father, and to tell me that she had shamefully succumbed to his relentless efforts to see her, just one last time. That night, she had gotten pregnant. My wife told me she wasn't sure who the father was, but she knew Michael wanted no part of being fingered as the baby's father if it was indeed his. Standing there in my living room just behind me, wearing his suit and tie, his hair neatly trimmed, his face closely shaven, Michael confirmed that, saying he would sign any papers, make any promise necessary for that information not to get out and ruin his relationship with his wife and two children.

Crushed to find out she had cheated on me and that she was pregnant, Erica tried to convince me the baby might've been mine. I knew that was impossible. She said she would never see Michael again, that she loathed the very sight of him, and only agreed to sleep with him that last time, to dangle in front of his face, the good thing he had lost. She told me I would be David's father: legally, and that role would never change.

It was nothing I wanted. It was the reason I had gone under the knife, severed any chance of creating another life, one that might've been taken from me like my first child. But something inside me saw it as an opportunity: a way to make good on the lousy job I did raising my daughter. I loved Erica, knew that she would not abort the baby, and knew she would only continue to accept me as her husband if I accepted her son as mine, so I agreed on the condition that Michael never see the baby, or Erica again: that he forever stay out of our lives. We all agreed, but yesterday he was in my living room.

I glanced at the clock on my dashboard, then up at my son in the rearview again.

"You ready to go to school, Lil' Man?"

"Yes, Dawdy," David said.

I got out, walked around truck, opened his door and attempted to unbuckle David from his car seat which always proved hilarious and a bit of a task.

"C'mon, Lil' Man," I said, struggling. He wrestled with me, shimmying in the seat, intentionally making it more difficult for me to pull him out. Finally succeeding, I grabbed him, his bag with all of his stuff, shouldered it and slammed the door shut with my hip. Walking him toward the door of the daycare building, he said, "Not taking me work with you, are you Dawdy?"

"Nah, buddy. Feel fortunate you have another twenty years or so before you have to deal with agony of work."

"Ag-gony?" David repeated.

"That's right, torture dude. Enjoy this time when all that's expected of you is not to poop your training diaper."

He laughed in my face, having no idea of what I was talking about.

This had been our ritual for the past six months, since he had turned two and Erica and I had enrolled him here. I was always the one to drop him off. This had been our time together: getting my son into the car, our conversations on the way, and then dropping him off. It made me happy, looking forward to this in the mornings, and I was sad every time I watched the daycare building shrink in my rearview as I drove away. It was our father-son time together. I loved it, didn't know what I would do without it.

As mothers and a couple of fathers walked past me on the sidewalk, nodding their heads or smiling and saying good morning, I greeted them back, my stride slowing until I came to a complete stop with David in my arms.

"Dawdy, what are we doing?" the boy asked, tired of standing in the middle of the sidewalk, the warm morning sun, roasting his face.

I thought about the question and again considered taking off. From Atlanta, the Florida border is roughly five hours. We'd be there before Erica returned home from work. And unlike last time when I had no job, and not even eight hundred dollars in the bank, I've been working straight for a few years and have thousands to draw from.

"Dawdy..." David was becoming increasingly impatient, squirming in my arms. "What we doing?"

I took a step toward the Volvo, thought another moment about our potential escape, then told myself as I turned back toward the daycare building, "What we're going to do is trust what your mommy keeps telling Dawdy: that there's absolutely nothing to worry about, and all will be fine."

3

I wasn't as attentive as I normally was during class this morning. I stood in front of the blackboard, writing addition, subtraction and multiplication problems, not caring that the kids were raising their hands, yelling out the answers. I was too busy thinking about what might've really been going on, if anything, behind my back regarding Michael.

"Mr. Foster, are you okay? Earth to Mr. Foster!" Jeremy Jenkins, a freckled face, redheaded boy, yelled out, causing all the kids to laugh and me to snap out of my trance.

"Yeah, sorry. Sorry, I'm fine I said, scribbling more problems on the board. "Won't happen again."

At lunch, I drove the fifteen minutes to my father's law offices. I took the elevator up to the 23rd floor, desperately needing to speak to him, needing his expert opinion.

My father was a prominent Atlanta attorney who ran a very successful and widely known law firm, representing much of the Atlanta's rich and famous. The raunchy cable station, Bravo was seriously considering doing a reality show about his firm, but backed out for unknown reasons at the last moment.

Inside my father's office, I paced back and fourth in front of his desk, nervously shaking my head, anticipating he'd tell me the worst news possible.

My father, Victor Roberts, was not twenty years older than me, was a handsome man with chiseled facial features, a head full of thick hair: graying around the temples and always neatly trimmed. He wore suits as expensive as some of the crappy cars driving around the poorer neighborhoods of Atlanta, tastefully colorful ties, and brilliant white shirts.

My father and I had two relationships: the one that spanned from the day I was born till I was roughly four years old, when he tucked tail and ran out of my life, and the relationship that started two years ago, after I had spent nights looking for him on line, finally tracking him down to his law offices, then having to go so far as to camp out in his waiting room with David, who was then a baby, hoping to get my father's attention, hoping that we could start again, have a relationship.

It was tough going. He pretended then as though he didn't know me, that I wasn't even his son. But after relentless pushing, he came around, softened up to David, and now my father is the proud grandfather, loves David almost as much as I do.

I forgave him for abandoning me, although it was nearly the hardest thing I've ever done. There were times when I'd think about how much of a better man I would be if he had been there to raise me, guide me, inform me. I'm doing okay for myself, but if he had stayed, I know I would've been an exponentially better husband, father...person.

"Do you see anything?" I asked, staring down at the papers spread out before him. He stood on the other side of his desk, reading glasses on, bending over the contracts I had snuck this morning from out of the home office safe Erica and I shared.

"I told you, Stan," my father said, looking at me from over the top of the glasses sitting propped on his nose. "Everything looks legitimate."

"Are you sure?"

Dad pulled the glasses off, set them aside on the desk. "What's this all about?"

Two years ago, after I told Dad how David was conceived, he thought I was a fool to stay with Erica. So now, for fear of appearing like a pushover in his eyes, I feared telling him what was happening between us.

"The father showed up yesterday. You know, David's biological father. The guy I told you about: Michael." The mention of the man's name, forcing me to relive the moment from yesterday after my wife told me to wait in the kitchen.

I did as she asked: closed myself behind the door, paced the ceramic tiles, sweat covering my brow, my mind going crazy with what she would tell me when she finally walked through that door. I knew she would tell me that she would take my son, leave me for the clown in the other room. That had to be it. There could be no other reason why she dismissed me, knowing the history between the three of us.

Telling myself to calm down, I grabbed the back of one of the kitchen chairs, dragged it out from under the table and settled into it. If Erica told me what I feared, I would have no choice but accept her not

29

wanting me; I would walk away with some dignity. But regardless of what she said, I was not giving that man my son.

When Erica pushed through the door, I stood from the chair like a man after the trial in which he knew he would be found guilty. She walked over, stopped in front of me. Her eyes and nose pink and irritated, she looked at me with a pain I had never seen before. I could tell she had been crying.

Yes, this was the day I dreaded, but in the back of my head, knew would always come. She would tell me it was Michael she truly loved. She was leaving me. She would take an overnight bag, but would be back on Monday with a moving truck for the rest of her belongings.

"It's okay," I said. "You don't have to say anything. I know what this is."

"What are you talking about?" Erica said, appearing so thrown that I felt maybe I was wrong.

"No...nothing. What happened out there?"

Her lips quivering, her eyes tearing, she tried to form a word, but could not speak. She dropped her head, fell into my chest and wrapped her arms around me. It felt as though her legs would give under her. I held her to me, then took her by her shoulders, looked into her eyes from arm's distance.

"Erica, what happened out there?"

"I...there..." she said, through tears running freely down her cheeks.

"Tell me!"

"A fire," she said sniffling.

"What? When?" I asked, those words being the last I expected to hear from her.

"This morning. Early. Michael came home to find his house burning."

My grip loosened on my wife. I staggered one step back, momentarily putting myself in his situation, wondering what I'd do if I had been faced with the horrifying reality of losing my family. "Is everyone—"

"They're dead, Stan." Eyes cold and unblinking, she said. "His entire family is dead."

I couldn't move. "How...how did it happen?"

"He came home around one in the morning, and the entire house was just burning. By the time the fire department came, it was...it was too late."

Back in Dad's office, returning from my thoughts, I looked up sadly at him and said: "He came to tell Erica his entire family died in a fire."

My father frowned, appeared sympathetic to the news, but said, "And?"

"And I'm fearing since his children are gone, since they're dead, he'll want back the one he gave away."

"Doesn't matter what he wants. He signed the contracts, Stan. There's nothing he can do now."

"And if for some reason, Erica wanted to give David back to him."

"Why would she do that?" Dad said, his tone insinuating I was acting as paranoid as Erica said I was.

"I'm not saying she would," I said, frazzled. "I'm just saying *if. If* she wanted to, could this man just swoop in a take David from me?

"I told you no, son. You're worrying for nothing. If he put his name on this," Dad said, lifting the pages from his desk, "There's no way it can be reversed unless you sign them back over to him."

I sighed, not feeling comforted in the least by what he just told me.

Staring at me with concern, Dad walked around the desk, stood face to face with me. "Look at me, son."

Feeling like a powerless child, I lifted my head.

"Something going on you not telling me about?"

"Marriage stuff, Dad." I shook my head, smiling stupidly. "Nothing, I'm sure, millions of other couples aren't going through this very minute."

He squeezed my shoulder. "That's right. And it'll pass."

"You sure?"

"Yes."

"And if it doesn't?"

He had been ready to release his grip on me, but hearing something very near fear in my voice, he left his hand there, waiting for me to say more. "I'm not going to walk away from my son just because things get tough with his mother. I'm not you." It was a low blow, but he deserved one every once in a while for leaving me when I was still wetting the bed and afraid of the dark.

"I know you're not," Dad said. "And I'll say again, I'm sorry for taking off, but that's in the past. All I can do is be here for you now, and you know I am, right?"

"I guess. Yeah." We stared at each other a second longer; I was thankful he was in my life now, even though the words I had just spoke said the opposite. I broke eye contact, turned and gathered up the contracts off his desk and stuffed them back in the folder they were in. "So I'm good then? Nothing to worry about?"

"No, son. But if something fishy does come up, you know you have my entire law firm at your disposal. There's no way we're going to lose David. You know how much I love him."

"Yeah." I did know that.

"And Janis too," he added as an after thought.

My father had met my 23 year-old daughter one time. I brought her to his office so she could finally meet her grandfather. He tried to make nice with her, but Janis's mother had already ruined my daughter's opinion of the man, telling her over and over again how he had abandoned me when I was just a boy. When Janis was finally given the opportunity to meet him, she smiled politely, but had little to say.

"How is she doing in school? She should be ready to graduate next month, right?" Dad asked now.

He was correct, she should've been. That was if Janis had stayed the course: the path to medical school, the future-doctor fast track to financial wealth, health and happiness. But my sweet daughter took a metaphorical wrong turn. Actually it was more like Janis mashed her foot on the gas, raced the car through a guardrail, sped off a cliff, and crashed and burned at the bottom of a ravine. But my father didn't need to know all that. Her recent failure was my cross to bear for not being there for her. I felt it was my fault her life was going to shit. But there was still time to stop that, at least I hoped.

"Yeah, Janis is fine. Still my genius, and ready to get her degree in a month, then off to medical school," I lied.

4

Bolstered by the assurance of my father telling me I had nothing to worry about, the afternoon at work was a bit better than this morning. After school let out, I walked to the faculty parking lot, climbed into my SUV and started toward daycare to pick up David. The thought of seeing him made me feel better, made me secure in that Erica and I would get through this gray area concerning Michael. What was on my mind now was the situation I chose not to tell Dad about concerning my daughter Janis. I made a left down a busy three-lane street still not certain how I'd help the girl get back on track and still not certain how she was able to undo all the good she had going for her.

My daughter had been on full academic scholarship, was getting good grades, was on her way to medical school, when all of a sudden, four months ago, she told her mother that she had flunked out. Two months after that, I get a phone call at three in the morning. It was Serena, frantic, screaming on the line, telling me I had to come to the house. I drove there, wearing my pajama shirt tucked into my jeans, picked her up, took her where she told me: the local police station where we bailed out my daughter who looked haggard, glassy-eyed and high from the drugs she supposedly had been in possession of.

I controlled my rage long enough for the three of us to seal ourselves in the car then I lost it, yelling into the back seat at Janis who was slumped over, leaning against the passenger door, eyelids low, long curly hair all over her head.

"Drugs?" I hollered, eyeing her through the rearview. "It's bad enough you flunked out of college! Now this! What has gotten into you?"

She said nothing. In the mirror, all I could see was one of her shoulders, her cheek fallen upon it, as though she was nodding off to sleep. I turned, threw an arm over my seat, grabbed her and shook her. "Janis, I'm tired of this! You need to tell me what happened."

"I don't know, Dad," she said, apathetic, in that teenage "Just relax and chill" tone that drives me fucking bananas. "You're ruining your life right now!" I yelled. "Dammit, you're going to tell—"

"It's a boy!" Serena said, intervening from the passenger seat. "It's some boy, Stan."

Still holding firmly to my daughter, I turned to my ex-wife. "What?"

"I'd met him a couple of months ago," Serena admitted. "He looked like bad news, like trouble. She's dating him."

"Why...why didn't you tell me?"

"I told her she needed to leave him alone. She told me she had, but by the looks of things," Serena took a glance to the back seat. "I'm assuming she hasn't."

It turned out the drugs belonged to the boy, but he had told my daughter to carry them just in case they got stopped. He already had two strikes against him, a third would put him away for ten years. My daughter foolishly went along, so she was arrested and he was allowed to walk away. After that incident, I demanded to meet the guy. That happened three days later. Serena and I sat in her kitchen, waiting for the boy's arrival. She had filled me in on what little she knew about him. He wasn't in school and didn't have a job.

"And you let her continue seeing him?" I questioned.

"She's 23, Stan. She's grown. I can't put her on punishment anymore like she's a child."

"But she lives under your roof!" I whispered harshly. Janis was in the living room, waiting for the boy to arrive as we were.

"And I'm trying to keep it that way," Serena whispered back, leaning across the table toward me. "We go too hard, we might drive her away. As long as she lives here, at least I can keep an eye on her, not have her running the street with that fool, getting arrested again."

We heard the doorbell ring and listened as Janis answered the door. Serena and I stood when we heard my daughter leading her new boyfriend down the hallway to us.

Janis stepped into the kitchen first, then the boy popped out from behind her. My jaw dropped. I stood speechless at what I saw: cornrowed hair, unkempt beard, lids laying low over cloudy eyes, as though the boy just took a few hits off a blunt standing outside the front door to prepare himself for this meeting. His jeans appeared three times too big, the bottoms spilling over into the open laces of black work boots. He was short: a few inches taller than my daughter's 5'4", but very muscular. If he were a dog, he'd be a Pit bull, probably one that was chained to the garage, left to sleep nights shivering in the cold, and served all his meals out of a an old hubcap.

37

"This is Rasul," Janis told me. She was smiling, proudly: smitten and in love. It was all over her face.

I turned to him, saw that he was extending an arm out to me; tattoos of skulls, marijuana leaves and spider webs spilled out from under his short sleeve, slinking all the way down to the knuckles on his fist.

I reluctantly took his hand, shook, and we sat down to talk.

Afterward, as Janis walked the boy back toward the front door, Serena and I came together. If we had been thinking the same thing throughout the half hour conversation we had with Rasul and Janis, almost at the same time, we said, "We have to get rid of him!"

Five minutes away from the daycare center, I was snatched from my thoughts by my ringing cell phone. I glanced down at it, saw Serena's name flashing across the screen. I answered the call, getting a strange feeling that something was wrong. "Hello," I said, hoping I was wrong.

"Stan!" Her voice shrill and panic-filled, I didn't have to hear another word to know that I was right and something was definitely wrong.

5

I slammed on the brakes in front of Serena's house, leaving the truck—one tire up on the curb—the door swinging open after I had jumped out. I ran across the grass toward the house, climbed the stairs and tried the knob first, even though I had a key. It turned.

Speeding over here, on the phone with Serena, I heard yelling and screaming in the background: my daughter's voice pleading, Rasul's voice yelling, and over the top of all that, Serena telling me, "He just went crazy, throwing things, saying he's going to hit Janis. Please, Stan! Get over here now!"

I whipped a U-turn, almost causing two separate accidents, and sped the ten minutes to the house.

Now, I stopped abruptly in the living room, taking in the devastation that lay at my feet: lamps toppled over onto the floor, the coffee table upended, the area rug flipped and bunched over in a corner, one of the blinds had been yanked from the front window and was stretched across the floor like an accordion. The room was deathly quiet. I looked up to see my ex-wife standing in a corner, her black hair pulled back in a pony tail, stressful sweat rolling in beads down her brown skin. Janis and the boy were in the center of the mess hugging as though just surviving a natural disaster.

Trying to stop the anger from building too quickly in me, I spoke slowly when I said, "Tell me what the hell is going—"

"Dad, I can explain," Janis started, speaking from the arms of the one I figured responsible for the ruin we were standing in.

"No!" I said, pointing a shaking finger at my daughter. "Serena," I lowered my voice a bit. "What happened?"

"Sir..." the boy interrupted. "It's my fault. If you'd allow me to explain," Rasul said, throwing me off by how properly and politely he spoke, which made me believe that once there might've been a decent boy under all that twisted hair, sagging clothes and scribbled ink.

"Speak," I said, deciding I'd give him exactly thirty seconds to make sense of the insanity I was looking at.

"First, Mr. Foster," Rasul said, tightening his embrace around Janis. "I love your daughter."

"I don't want to hear that. You're supposed to be explaining this shit to me. Do it. You have twenty seconds."

The boy swallowed hard, released Janis, shoved both his fists into his sagging jeans pockets, the muscles in his beefy forearms twitching with the movement. He looked down at his boots like a bashful child. "I thought Janis was—"

"Look at me when you talk to me," I ordered.

He looked up meeting my eyes. He tried to appear compliant, submissive, as though he knew his place in this situation, but I sensed that was an act.

"I thought Janis was cheating on me."

"I wasn't, Dad!" Janis spoke up, as though it mattered to me.

"Janis, quiet," I said. "And..." I said, focusing my attention back on the boy. "You thought that you could come in here and destroy this house because—"

"I was wrong, Mr. Foster, about everything. And I apologize. I will clean all this up. I just love—"

"Shut up," I said, holding up a finger. "Don't tell me about how much you think you love—"

"But I do love her."

"I said I don't want to hear—"

"But Mr. Foster—"

I hurried over to the boy, stopped right in front of him, looked him eye to eye. "Did you hear what I said?"

He stared back, his chest heaving: the boy taking such big breaths I could practically hear the air whooshing out of his nostrils. His eyes were narrowed as though he resented me being in his face, as though he thought I was embarrassing him in front of my daughter, and he didn't appreciate it. I looked down, saw his hands clenched into fists, noticing the likeness of spikes tattooed onto each of his knuckles.

"Rasul, is there a problem?" I asked with authority.

He continued staring me in the eyes without answering.

"How old are you?" I asked.

"Twenty four, sir."

"A grown man."

He nodded.

"Then act like one, and if there's a problem, tell me and we'll work it out like men," the tone in my voice suggesting I had no problem stepping outside, fighting on the front lawn.

"No, sir. No problem."

"Good," I said taking a final step toward him, lowering my voice so only he could hear. "Because if you ever put your hands on my daughter, I will find you, and I will kill you," I said, poking him in the space between his pectorals; he felt like a granite slab. "You understand me?"

"Yes, sir."

"No," I said, leaning close enough for him to feel the warmth of my breath on his cheek when I said, "You answered too quickly. I want you to think about what I said. Take a moment, consider what it would be like to no longer be living, to feel yourself dying while I'm beating the life out of you. Think about how your mother will feel when she finds your body in the vacant lot where I dump it."

Rasul stared menacingly at me, chewing on the inside of his mouth. "My mother is dead, sir."

"Then the two of you will be reunited if you ever do anything like this again. Now do you understand?"

He paused a moment as if for thought, then said, "I understand, sir."

"Good, now get the hell out of this house."

"Daddy!" Janis shouted her disproval.

"Janis, not now!" I said.

"But Daddy, you can't—"

"Janis, I said not now."

"It's cool, baby," Rasul said to her, immediately diffusing the situation. My daughter obediently backed down at his request, making me wonder exactly what kind of control he had over her.

6

Janis, Serena and I were at the kitchen table fifteen minutes after Rasul left, trying to make some sense out of what just happened.

Janis cast her eyes away from both me and her mother, as though she were alone in the room. I glanced at Serena for help. She hunched her shoulders, letting me know she was as clueless of what to do as I was.

I sighed. "Janis, this is my fault, isn't it?"

Janis cut an eye back at me, then looked away again.

"You can be honest. Everything that's going on, you failing out of school, the stuff with the police, and this...this boy. It's because I left you when you were younger. Is that right?"

Janis faced me. Still appearing angry, she said, "You didn't leave me. Mom took me from you." She cut her eyes at her mother. Serena rolled her eyes back.

"I know, but I allowed it to happen. I could've fought harder for you, but I didn't."

"Dad," Janis said, her tone now sympathetic. "It wasn't your fault. I told you that."

"Well, I appreciate that," I told my daughter, not sure if she has truly forgiven me for my absence. "Now regarding what happened with that boy, it's never going to happen again."

"I know," Janis said. "Rasul said—"

"Doesn't matter what Rasul said, because you're done with him. It's over."
 You're not seeing him anymore."

"But, Daddy!"

"Stan..." I heard Serena say.

I turned around. "It's over!" I told both of them.

"Stan, maybe we should—"

"Serena, I told you already—"

"Mom!" Janis appealed to her mother who had stood, walked over to Janis and coaxed her out of the chair.

"Go on upstairs," Serena said, smoothing her hand across our daughter's back as she escorted her toward the door. "I'm going to talk to your father a while."

When Serena turned back to me, my arms were crossed, my face crumpled in a furious scowl. "Tell me what the hell you're doing. The boy tore up your house and—"

"And I told you, you tell Janis she can't see him anymore, all that's going to do is make her want to be with him more."

"You're okay with them being together? Is that what you're telling me."

"Hell no, Stan. You know me better than that," Serena said, falling into one of the kitchen chairs, throwing her head back. She closed her eyes.

"Then you're suggesting what?" I said, standing over her.

My ex-wife opened her eyes and lifted her head. "We have to make him leave her."

"And exactly how do we do that?"

"From what Janis said, he has nothing. He sure as hell looks like that's the case. I don't know. We bribe him to leave our daughter. We give him more money than he's ever seen, and we tell him never to see Janis again."

7

After leaving Serena's, I called the daycare, told them that I'd be picking up David later than usual. I needed a drink and time to sort out the mess that was clogging my brain. I called my best friend Pope of twelve years and told him to meet me at one of our favorite bars on Ponce.

A trio of flat screens hung over the bar playing sports on two of them, financial news on the other. Foo Fighters screamed from hidden speakers, while mostly men and a handful of women, all of them obviously coming straight from work—still in suites and skirts—sat at the bar talking over glasses of liquor and beer.

After already having two shots of bourbon, I slammed down my empty glass on the wooden bar and flagged down the balding bartender for another.

"You okay, Stan?" Pope, a big guy with a deep voice and better than average looks, asked. He was married since before I met him, and was the father of two girls, and eight and a six year old.

I ignored the question while I watched the bartender—his beefy hand around the neck of the bottle—pour my third shot. I quickly lifted the glass he presented, kicked it back, nearly choking on the burn of the alcohol going down.

"One more before you put it back," I winced.

"Stan!" Pope said, grabbing my wrist in mid reach of my fourth shot. "What's going on with you?"

Already tipsy and having to catch myself from toppling off the bar stool, I spun to face him. Knowing I could trust him with anything and everything I told him. He was my counsel, my buddy, my trusted advisor.

"Janis's quote unquote boyfriend," I said, drunkenly doing the air quote thing with my fingers, "...tore up Serena's house. I thought I was about to kick his ass."

"He didn't touch Janis, did he?" Pope's eyes were wide awaiting the answer.

"His bloody head would be sitting on this bar between us if he had."

Shaking his head, Pope said, "I feel you, cause if some fool dared even think about putting his hands on either of my little girls, I'd be in prison for man slaughter."

I laughed off what he said. "Yeah, right." Pope, to be as big as he was—6 foot tall, 230 pounds—was the most gentle of giants. I couldn't count the times he avoided physical violence in one bar or another, initiated by drunken men Pope could've squashed like bugs, because he was all about non-violent resolution and talking things out like gentlemen. "Manslaughter, yeah. You're the most law biding, cotton puff I know."

Pope grabbed his glass, brought it to his lips, slowly letting the golden amber liquid drain into his mouth, then set his beer down, turned to me and said in all seriousness, "Let some dude, now or ever, try to get crazy with my daughters, swear to God, hope to die, stick a fucking needle in my eye, I would kill him, and I would understand if you did the same."

8

I had picked David up, carried him home, wishing Janis was as easy to care for and control as my two and half year old son.

Before I left the bar, Pope asked me how Erica was, how things were going with the "Michael situation", which he said was not really a situation at all, just Michael realizing what a good thing he had in Erica, and after all he's lost, wishes he had her back.

"He wishes that about his son, too," I said.

"Your son, Stan. David is *your* son," Pope said, softly hitting me in the shoulder with a fist. "Nothing will ever change that. Got it?" He smiled as though just willing it would make it so.

I wasn't sure about that, but said, "Yeah, got it." He gave me hug. We clapped each other, loud and rather hard on the backs, then went our separate ways.

At home, I helped Erica make dinner: I peeled potatoes, set the table and entertained David while she did all the real cooking. At the dinner table, I sat quiet, picking at the food she made, nodding my head and giving one-word answers to conversations she tried to start.

"Stan, you okay? I heard Erica ask.

I nodded, pushed some of the mash potatoes around on my plate then set my fork down. "Remember all the stuff I told you about that boy my daughter is dating?"

"Yeah."

"There's more," I said, filling her in on everything that had happened earlier.

"So you were by your ex-wife's house?"

"Yeah. She called me. Dude was losing it," I said, thinking it odd what she focused on, even though I told her Rasul nearly torn down the house with his bare hands.

Her tone polite, but attitudinal, she asked, "Isn't there someone else your ex-wife could've called? I mean, she's seeing someone right?"

"I don't know what she's doing. Maybe."

"Then why couldn't she have called him?"

"Because it was Janis's boyfriend that was going ape shit at Serena's house, and Janis is my child, not whatever guy Serena might be dating."

"I got you," Erica said, looking down at her plate as she cut another piece of her pork chop. "But you have a child over here to take care of."

I stopped myself from saying the first thing that came to mind, because it would've been something about her having her nerve telling me about my responsibilities to my son, when more times than not, she referred to David as only hers. "Lately, it seems as though you don't trust me to take care of him."

"And you say that because I insist you get decent tires on your truck? I just want our baby to be safe."

"It's more than that, and you know it," I said, pushing my plate aside. "Things aren't the way they used to be, and I'm wondering if it has anything to do with that man being in my house yesterday."

"No," Erica said, shaking her head. "No Stan. It doesn't and I don't want to fight with you. We've done way too much of that lately." She scooted from her chair to the one next to me, and took my hand. "Go upstairs, take a shower and relax. I'll put David down and be up to give you something to take your mind off of all of this."

9

My head spun as I lay under my wife's gyrating hips. I was breathless as I stared dizzily up at her bouncing breasts and her full lips as she moaned my name. It had been forever since she had initiated sex, and even longer since she was involved as she was that moment. She lowered herself to me, pressing her mouth to mine, slipping her tongue into between my lips as she rode me harder, attempting to force me to climax.

"Come for me, baby," she urged, her voice soft and wet in my ear.

We had been making love for half an hour. I missed it so much, I didn't want it to end. "No," I moaned back, grabbing tighter to the flesh of her ass, knowing I had no real say in the matter.

Not accepting my answer, she took charge, tightening her vaginal muscles around me, rolling her hips in just the right way to massage what she wanted out of me. Beaten down, unable to fight any longer, I conceded, erupting into her: my back spontaneously arching as I plunged deeper into her, triggering an orgasm of her own. She screamed, as she always did when it was a good one, grabbed tight to me, bore down harder, absorbing the waves of warm fluid that exploded into her. We lay there afterward, her body heavy on top of mine, both of us spent, our hearts banging against the others. She rolled off, lay on her back, enjoying the cool air of the ceiling fan blades lazily spinning over us.

Her head on my chest, I played in the tangles of her hair like I used to do when we were first married, before there was any of this Michael drama, and before Erica had snuck off and gotten pregnant by him.

"That was so good," she breathed, turning, kissing me on the chest.

I nodded in agreement as though she could see. She rolled, kneeled over me and kissed my lips. "I'm gonna take another quick shower."

I watched her climb out of bed, her body even more beautiful as the day we met: the little bit of weight she kept on from giving birth to our son, inflated everything to perfection. She stopped before walking out the door.

"Wanna join me?" she asked.

I smiled. "Don't think I have the strength to climb out of bed, you put it on me so good. You go ahead."

"Your loss," she smiled.

"I know." I continued smiling, but once she was gone, I let my head fall back into the pillow, and the smile immediately drained from my face. I lay out across the bed, fighting a losing war, attempting to stop thoughts of Michael from invading my mind at the worst times: like right after making love to my wife. Staring at the strip of light from under the bathroom door, hearing the shower water running behind it, I told myself Michael had no business visiting my house, but I guess I understood why Erica told me to wait in the kitchen. It was a delicate moment, one in which she didn't want me going off in a jealous rage, asking why he was in my home again? Why he couldn't he go home and be with his own family, when in fact, he no longer had either, because his house lay in ashes, and his family had been burned to death.

I heard the shower water stop in the bathroom, the metallic scrape of the shower curtain rings slide across the rod. Erica stepped out a moment later—white bath towel wrapped around her body, droplets of water clinging to the ends of her hair—and into our room, stopping just in front of the bed.

"Can I get back in with you?" She asked, smiling seductively.

"Yeah, but the towel has to go," I said, trying not to let my thoughts ruin the nice night we were having.

She unfastened the knot, let the towel fall to her feet, did a little naked shimmy, then jumped into bed with me smelling of lilac and passion fruit shower gel. We lay together, spooning: my arms wrapped around her, holding hands, my chin hung over her shoulder, her hair in my face, brushing soft against my cheek.

I told myself I didn't care about Michael's loss. That was because I hated him for how he's made himself a part of my life. But his family was innocent, and despite how slimy a man Michael was, they didn't deserve what they had gotten, which led me to ask my wife, "Do...do they know how the fire was started?" I assumed if Michael had heard, he would've told Erica.

"I..."Erica started, her back still to me. She sounded surprised that I would ask. "He hasn't...said anything to me about it."

"So you're talking to him?"

Erica didn't answer, but attempted to pull out of our embrace to face me. I held her tight, stopping her. "You don't have to get up to tell me whether or not—"

"Just..." she struggled. "I just need to look you in the face when I talk to you about this."

She sat up in front of me, her legs folded, pulling the comforter over her naked thighs and breasts. "There's nothing going on, Stan. If that's what you're worried—"

"I didn't say there was," I said sitting up on my elbows. "I just asked if you were talking to him."

"Yes. But the only reason is because his family died, and he needs someone to talk to."

"Must that someone be you? I mean it's not like you have the power to bring them back to life. Or do you?"

Erica shook her head, making a face, not appreciating my comment. "I've known him for ten years and—"

"You mean you were fucking him for ten years. You were his mistress for ten years. Now what? You're his grief counselor? Make me understand, Erica," I said, raising my voice. "You said it was over!"

"It is!" she said, raising her voice to match mine.

"Then why can't he just fucking leave you alone?" I yelled.

"Because he wants me to go the funeral tomorrow!"

I was floored. I sat speechless, staring at my wife, wondering if she knew the damage she was doing to us. I threw the comforter off me, jumped out of bed, paced across the floor, shaking my head. "No. No way you're going to that funeral!"

"Stan—"

"No!" I spun, facing her. "Why does he need *my* wife to be at a funeral for *his* family?"

"What if you were in that situation?"

"You mean if I had fucked someone else's wife, gotten her pregnant, had a baby by her, and came home in the middle of the night from who the hell knows where, to find this house burning down with you and David inside?" I looked at Erica, waiting for her to confirm that's what she was talking about. When she didn't, I said, "I don't like to imagine that, Erica. But if it actually happened, I wouldn't be alive right now. If I had been in that motherfucker, Michael's shoes, I would've run in this house with it burning, falling the fuck down, collapsing in on itself. I would've ran in here, even if I knew there was no way I'd make it out. Because I couldn't live with myself knowing I hadn't tried to save my family."

Erica sat in the middle of the bed, appearing mildly touched by my confession, then went back on defense for the man she seemed to sympathize with more than me. "That's not the guy he is," Erica said. "But it doesn't change the fact that his family is dead, and he asked me to go pay my respects."

I paced away again. "I can't believe you," I said, but then spun around, struck by a thought. "Is that why...is that why you were so nice tonight? Why we had sex, because you were hoping I'd say yes to this?"

"No. Of course not!" my wife said, shaking her head: exaggerated sweeps to the left and right, as though outraged I'd even consider that.

I walked back over to her, no longer believing a word she said. "What is it with him, huh? You say you're not still—"

"I'm not!"

"Then what? You still in love with him?"

Unblinking, she stared me in the eyes for a beat then said, "No, Stan."

"Is there something you're not telling me? Is he trying to win you back?"

"No."

"How do you know?"

"He's leaving, okay," Erica said. I tried to detect any sadness in her words but couldn't. "He has nothing left here, so he gave notice at his job and said he's moving to D.C."

"When?" I asked, wanting him gone as soon as possible. I would've offered him help packing, split half the time driving the U-Haul to our nation's capital if I thought that'd get him out of our lives sooner.

"I don't know. But I'm not going to ignore the fact that I had something with him for ten years. The man's family is dead. He asked me to attend the funeral. I want to do that for him."

"And I'm saying you can't. You will not go to that funeral. Do you understand?"

"And what if I do?" Erica asked.

That was a question I wasn't prepared to answer, because I had no answer. "Go, and you'll find out."

10

I was at my ex-wife's door early the next morning, the sky was still dark outside when I stepped inside holding the two cups of Dunkin Donuts coffee.

This morning while was shaving, my cell phone vibrated on the bathroom shelf. The faucet water running, the phone pressed to my ear, I listened as Serena told me she needed to see me that morning, that it was an emergency, and if possible could I call in sick today.

"So what's all this about?" I asked Serena, handing her the coffee with extra cream and Splenda—how she always took it.

"Just go in the kitchen. There's something I need to show you. We can talk then."

I had expected to see Janis sitting at the table, maybe in her pajamas , drying her eyes after the huge blowout she just had with her mother, but there was no sign of my daughter. I pulled a chair, sat down, a crumple of folded tissue on the other side of the table, drawing my attention.

"Want anything? Juice? eggs? I can cook if you're hungry," Serena said.

"No, I'm fine. Just tell me why I'm missing a day of work? Is it something to do with Janice? That boy didn't come back, did he?"

Serena took a seat. She wore leggings and a black tank. She stared at me as though about to make a world-ending confession, her hands wrapped around the Styrofoam coffee cup as if to warm them. "Rasul hasn't been back, but he will be."

"You say that as though you're sure of it. Why?"

Serena's hand was on the wad of tissue I had spotted earlier. She slid it over in front of me. "Open it."

I dug into the paper and uncovered a pink, plastic pregnancy wand, a little window in the center of it, displaying two faint lines. I hadn't a clue of what they meant, but figured if two lines meant someone was not having a baby, the wand would've been at the bottom of the bathroom trashcan and not in front of me.

I looked up at Serena. "Please tell me this belongs to you."

Serena didn't answer, just gave me a look that said I must've been out of my mind.

Moments later, I climbed the stairs to the second floor, Serena behind me, telling me how the discovery came about: that Janis had been acting weird and when Serena asked her why did she seem she couldn't live without the boy, Janis got silent, then burst into a fit of sobs, tears and crazy woman theatrics. Serena sped to the closest CVS, bought the test, dragged Janis into the bathroom, and demanded she pull down her pants that very moment.

In front of Janis's bedroom door, Serena yanked on my arm, turned me to face her, stopping me from going in.

"Look, we have to be delicate with this, okay," she cautioned.

"Delicate?"

"Yes, delicate. Our daughter made a stupid mistake."

"One more in a string of them," I said.

"But she's still our daughter. Assuming we don't want to alienate her, have her running to that boy, we need to be careful how we handle this, okay."

"Yeah, okay," I grunted, turning the knob and pushing into the room.

Janis was up, sitting on the edge of the bed, face in her hands, wearing pajama bottoms and a t-shirt. I stood looking down at her, wanting to yell at her, frighten some sense into her, snatch her up, shake loose whatever was clouding her brain. Instead, I sat beside her and put an arm around my daughter. "It's all going to be all right."

"Is it?" She asked without looking up at me.

"When were you going to tell us?"

"I don't know...if ever."

I glanced up at Serena. She stood leaning against the doorframe, arms crossed, shaking her head.

"Really?" I said, trying to remain calm. "I'm not mad at you. We're not mad at you."

Janis looked up at her mother, my eyes following hers.

"She's not?" Janis asked.

"No," I said. "We just want to know what the plan is."

"What plan?" Janis asked.

"You're no longer in school. You're not working, and when you go looking for employment, you'll have the issue of that marijuana possession on your record. You're twenty-three years old. There's plenty of time to put things back on track. But this guy: he's bad news, and—"

"Hold it!" Janis said, scooting away from me. "I'm not leaving Rasul. I love him. We love each other. And we're having a baby."

"I don't know if that's such a good—"

"Janis," Serena said, interrupting me. "Your father is just saying that you and this boy might be too young—"

"How hold were you and Dad when you had me?" Janis was up from the bed again. "Younger than me and Rasul. And everything turned out fine."

"We had problems," I said. "I couldn't find work. We got divorced. You remember all that. Do you want the same to happen to the two of you?"

"So you should've aborted me?" Janis said. "Is that what you're saying?"

"No!" Serena said, walking over, taking Janis's other hand. "That's not what—"

"It doesn't matter," Janis cried. "I'm not doing it. Rasul and I are in love! Our baby was conceived from love!"

"Janis," I said, taking her hand, trying to reel her in and comfort her. "Maybe you just need to calm down and—"

"No, Dad!" Janis said, yanking away from me, smearing tears from her face. "Like you said, I'm 23. I'm grown. I can do what I want, and I don't care what either of you say, I'm staying with Rasul, and we're having our baby!"

11

At a little after 3 PM that same afternoon, Serena and I sat on the same side of a Waffle House booth. An old couple sat gumming scrambled eggs and grits in the booth in front of us. Three other diners sat at the bar hunched over cups of coffee and juice, while employees in paper hats and aprons slid across the greasy work station floor, frying up orders. Opposite us was Rasul, his hair freshly cornrowed, his beard newly trimmed; he wore a collared shirt as though for a job interview. He sat with his tatted hands folded on the table, and only then did I see the old healed scars under fresh scabs on his knuckles, as though he was into punching brick walls for stress relief.

This morning, after Janis went off on me and her mother, Serena turned to me. "Why don't you leave us alone for a moment, okay?"

"But—"

"Just go downstairs, Stan. I'll be down in a sec."

"Yeah, okay."

Fifteen minutes later, Serena pulled out the kitchen chair in front of me, and sat down.

"So?" I said.

"So I got the boy's phone number. I told Janis if she's going to be with him, if they're going to have a baby together, you and I should have a long talk with him."

"I'm not talking to that boy about how he's going to ruin my daughter's life."

"Neither am I. We're going to find out what it'll take for him to leave her alone."

In the Waffle House restaurant, Rasul picked up his complementary glass of water and took a sip. "I'm glad you asked me to meet you two, Ms. Foster." His tone was proper and polite, as always, it seemed. "And I apologize again for the mess I made of your house."

"That's happened. It's over with," I said. "There are more important things to talk about. You've gotten my daughter pregnant. I'm sure you're aware of that."

The boy chuckled, looked away bashfully, then back at us, a childish smile on his face.

That was the last reaction I expected from him. "What's funny?" I said. "Is there something funny about all of this?"

I felt Serena's hand clamp tight around my thigh under the table, reminding me that I had promised to keep my cool on the drive over, that we didn't want to scare the boy away or have him shut down on us so he wouldn't be open to the offer we were going to make him.

"I'm sorry, Mr. Foster," Rasul said, wiping the smirk off his face. "Yes sir, I know that's she's pregnant. Janis told me last week, and I told her we needed to let you guys know, but she was afraid of how you would react, so I let her decide when we'd do it. But I told Janis that you," he said, looking at Serena, "would find out anyway. That's just how mother's are."

"So we're gonna cut straight to the chase," I said, tired of the boy's voice in my ears. "You might be a nice young man, but I don't like you. I don't trust you, but I will respect you as a man and ask that you leave my daughter alone."

The smile was back on Rasul's face, his lips parted slightly as though waiting for me to finish before he responded.

"We need for you to end things with Janis," Serena said, politely finishing for me.

"But…" Rasul said. "She's having my baby. Have you talked to her about this?"

"You don't have to worry about our daughter. She'll be fine," I said.

Rasul looked around the small, windowed restaurant as though looking for the hidden camera and game show host to let him know he was being punked. He turned back to Serena and I. "But she's having our baby."

"I told you, that's not your problem," I said.

"But it's my baby," Rasul said. "I *am* concerned, and with all due respect, Mr. and Ms. Foster, I ain't going nowhere."

This was the response Serena and I figured we'd get while pulling up in the parking lot of Bank of America. We both had accounts there.

Before walking in, she asked, "So, final number: what do you think it'll take?"

"You said he has nothing. I don't know…two grand?" I guessed.

"Wouldn't that be nice," Serena said, looking through her purse for her bankcard. "I guess the more important question is, what is him leaving our daughter alone worth to us?"

69

In the Waffle House, Rasul said, "You two telling me that me and Janis won't work, I guess, is the reason you all asked me here. If that's the case, we don't have anything else to talk about." He took a last sip from his glass of water.

Serena looked frantically over at me as though we were losing him. He started to push his way out the booth.

"We have money!" Serena said louder than she needed, drawing the attention of a large woman, and her rotund child from the breakfast bar. Serena pulled a small, tightly packed envelope from her purse and slapped it on the table.

"$5,000, if you end things with Janis right now and never show your face around her again."

12

Serena and I celebrated our victory over a couple of margaritas and a basket of tortilla chips in a dark, Mexican cantina off Memorial Drive. We sat at the bar sipping sides of tequila with lime.

"If I had known it would've been that easy, I would've given the boy money the day after I met him," Serena joked.

After the Waffle House offer had been made, Rasul stood, his eyes locked on the envelope. He slid back into the booth.

"In there is five grand?" He said, never taking his eyes away. "Can I see it?"

"Of course," Serena said, sliding the envelope forward. "You can have it, but you call her tonight and let Janis know it's over. We have a deal?" she said, not removing her hand from the package.

To his credit, the boy gave it at least a moment of thought, appeared to have had the slightest bit of hesitation regarding dumping the girl he supposedly loved for a chunk of money, but said, "Yeah, Mr. and Mrs. Foster. It's a deal."

At the bar, Serena and I were both pretty tipsy and excited, toasting and laughing, until I lowered my glass and asked, "Have we thought about how this is going to affect Janis? If she loves this boy like she says, she's going to be heart broken, right?"

"She'll get over it," Serena said, reaching over, grabbing my glass and pushing it back in my hand. "Better heartbroken without Rasul, than blissful with him. Yes?"

"Hell yes," I agreed. "But there's still a baby. What about that?"

"Janis is an adult. It's her choice to make. She chooses to have the baby, we'll support her in that decision. If she decides not to, we'll support as well."

"Yeah, okay."

Serena raised her glass, urging me to do the same. I did, tapping mine against hers before we both turned the drinks up, then set the glasses back down on the bar.

"Bright side is," Serena said. "If Janis has the baby, your son David will have a little cousin to play with."

"If he's still my son?" I said, trying to play off what I said with a chuckle. She had already known about the fire, about Michael's family dying it in. Only now did I fill her in about him wanting Erica to go the funeral.

"She actually going to go?" Serena asked.

I glanced at my watch. "It's a little after five now. I told her she couldn't, but she might've said to hell with me. If so, she's there right now."

"You wanna call her and see?"

"Not really," I said, thinking that what I didn't know wouldn't hurt me. "If she's there, what can I do about it?"

No response from Serena. When I looked up, she was standing, leaning on the edge of her stool, shaking her head, sympathetically.

"What?" I asked.

"You look like you need a hug."

"Maybe. I don't know."

"Can I give you one?" Serena asked, wrapping her arms around me before I could stop her. Her arms tight around my neck, I pressed my face against her hair, felt myself hugging her back. I could barely hear her over the Mexican music blaring from the jukebox in the corner, when she asked softly, "Do you ever wonder if it's all worth it?"

Not wanting to move from the embrace, I asked, "If what's worth it?"

Serena pulled away only enough to look me in the eyes. "Everything you've been through with this woman. It's been a lot, Stan."

"I know, but—"

"The second guessing, the uncertainty—do you even know what she's doing?"

"Regarding what?"

"That other man? The boy, David?

"You mean my son."

"Is he, Stan? Is that how you really feel? Is he your son, like Janis is your daughter? Or is he your son because Erica is just allowing him to be?"

13

I walked in the house buzzing from my outing with Serena. It was approaching seven o'clock. Down the hall I saw that the kitchen light was on, and heard Erica in there baby-talking David. I smelled something cooking: beef of some kind.

I took steps toward the kitchen, but stopped near the stairs, torn between the options of greeting my dysfunctional family or just walking up the stairs, crawling into bed and not confronting what might've been a very ugly situation with my wife.

I placed a hand on the banister, took the first step, but looked back over my shoulder for some reason and caught a glimpse of something on the living room coffee table. I walked over, stared down at what was the program for Michael's family funeral. There was a grainy black and white photo of the three deceased on the cover. Michael's wife was more attractive than I had imagined. She was smiling and beautiful as she held a laughing boy and girl in her arms: kids appearing something near eight and ten years old at the time.

So Erica went to the funeral even after I asked her not to. I looked toward the kitchen, wondered if she accidently left this here, if she planned on keeping it a secret, planned to lie, tell me she had just gone to work and returned home? Or did she come in from the funeral and lay this here so I would see it when I walked in.

"You hungry? I made a roast," Erica said.

The funeral program in my hand, I turned to see her standing behind me. I made no effort to hide pamphlet. Erica glanced down at it, then back at me.

"So you went?" I asked.

"I did," she said, offering no apology.

"Even though I told you I didn't want you to."

"I told you why I felt I needed to. And—"

"And what?" I said, believing there could be no worse news left to give me.

"And I took David."

I gasped, imagining my young son in a room among praying, tearful and crying mourners dressed in black, three dead bodies laid out on display. I wondered had he been scared.

"So Michael could see him? That's why you took him?"

"I took him because I wanted him there with me," Erica said, seeming offended that I suggested it was for any other reason.

"So Michael didn't see David? He didn't talk to my son? Is that what you're telling me?"

"He came over, said 'hi' to him, shook his hand. He tried to talk to him longer, but I stopped him. Told him it wasn't a good idea."

"Really, Erica?" I said, walking up, infuriated. I pointed a finger between her eyes. "You know, you're full of shit." I turned and headed toward the front door. Erica was behind me, grabbing me by the arm, turning me to face her.

"Where are you going?"

76

"What do you want, Erica?" I yelled, not answering her question. "What the fuck are you doing? You don't love me anymore?"

"Of course I do!"

"Do you want a divorce? You want to leave me for him?"

Her eyes wide with surprise, she appeared as though she had no earthly idea of why I'd ask her such a thing. "No!"

"Really, Erica? Really?" I snatched my arm away from her, grabbed the doorknob and threw the front door open.

"His whole fucking family died in a fire, Stan!" Erica screamed, stopping me, halfway out the door. I had only stopped there because I could hear the pain and hurt in my wife's voice. There were tears on her face. "If you lost me and David the same way, and Janis was out there, never having met you, wouldn't you want to at least to see her once?"

"You shouldn't care what Michael wants. He's not your husband, I am. And David is no longer his son. He's mine." I stepped out the out the house, was about to slam the door shut, when Erica told me to wait.

"What is it?"

"I...I," Erica hesitated, combing fingers through her hair, looking down.

"Say it! Just say it, Erica," I said, frustrated, imaging there was nothing worse that could come out of her mouth than what she had already told me.

"I'm not saying it should be considered, but Michael is requesting visitation rights for David."

14

Pope sat in the leather easy chair off to my right, a beer in his fist, nodding sympathetically. We were in his basement. There was a 60 inch flat screen hanging over the fireplace, a pool table to the left, a stocked bar to the right and a handful of Atlanta Hawks and Falcons jerseys hanging from the walls: all of them signed.

Pope leaned further forward in his chair. "So what are you going to do?"

"Not grant him fucking visitation rights, if that's what you're asking me." I took a huge gulp of the second beer Pope had given me. Neither of them was having an effect on me. It wasn't strong enough. "Hell, is he even entitled? I have to ask my father about that."

"Does Erica want to give them to him?"

The bottle of beer turned completely vertical, I drained the last half of it as though it was water, then set the bottle down. "She says she has no interest in that, or him, but I think she might be lying."

"Erica wouldn't do that to you."

"How the fuck would you know, Pope? Are you married to her?"

"No."

"Right. Then you don't know. The last six months...they just...they haven't been the same. It's like she's gotten tired of me, like I'm something she tolerates, and sometimes I think she regrets the fact that she allowed me to adopt David."

"You don't know that."

"Every decision I make regarding David, she second guesses. Whenever I take him anywhere, she damn near demands I call or text her to let her know we made it safely. Then has the nerve to require updates during the day, and calls me pissed if I don't deliver them. She treats me like nothing more than his baby sitter, and I'm getting fucking tired of it! Throwing this clown Michael in the middle of everything, just makes things worse."

"How much of her behavior do you think he's responsible for?"

I paused to think after just twisting off the cap of another bottle of beer. "A lot. I don't know." I shook my head, took a swig. "I trust that she hasn't been, but for all I know, she could've been seeing him off and on since David was born. And now that his family is gone, maybe he feels the right to just come in and take my family from me."

"Then you have to take that away from him."

"What do you mean, take it away?" I said, my words slurring a bit.

Pope got up from his seat, stood in front of me. "You're the man in control. You're Erica's husband, you're David's father, and this Michael guy is not respecting that. You have to confront him. Let him know that's not gonna fly."

"I don't even know how to find him. What should I do, ask Erica for—"

"No," Pope said, getting up in my face. "You don't ask permission to speak to him. "Erica needs to know nothing about it. This is a matter between you and him. You find him and tell him to back the fuck off, or else."

"Fine," I said leaning back in my chair, cradling the bottle of beer in my palms. "I'll do it. I don't know exactly how, but I'll find him and I'll tell him to back the fuck off."

Pope went back to his chair, stared at me from there, as if concerned I wouldn't follow through. "It's the only way he'll stop, you know: is if you stop him."

"I know," I sighed.

There was a long, uncomfortable pause, during which I felt Pope still staring at the side of my face.

"How's that situation with your daughter and her boyfriend?" Pope asked, mercifully breaking the silence.

My mood lightened a bit, telling Pope how Serena and I handled things. "It worked like a charm."

"This probably won't be the end of him," Pope said, sounding sorry to disappointment me again. "I know people like him. Asking them to do something in exchange for money is like asking a crack whore to leave the drugs alone, then rewarding her with drugs whens she says she will."

I shut my eyes and shook my head. "I don't have time for analogies, Pope. Make it plain!"

"The boy is broke. He'd tell you he'd kill his own mother if you offered him five gees. But would he actually do it?"

"This guy probably would," I said.

Pope chuckled a little. My face remained stone-like.

"Dude's that bad, huh?"

"I think he might be."

"Give me his name," Pope said. "I have a buddy on the police force. He can run him through the system. If he's who you say he is, maybe something will pop up."

15

I came back home, feeling as though I'd rather be anywhere else, but knowing I needed answers to all the questions swirling in my head. After pushing the door closed, I pressed my forehead against it, taking a moment to calm down, fully accept the weight of my worsening situation. The room was dark around me. I assumed that was my wife letting me know she didn't care that I was out or when I came back. I'm sure she had already gone through her nightly ritual of fixing dinner, feeding David, bathing him, tucking him in, then coming downstairs, having a glass of wine and stare off into her thoughts before going up to bed. I hadn't received a phone call or a text from her asking where I was, or when I was coming back, leading me to believe that maybe she was trying to get accustomed to nights without me.

"Get out of your fucking head, Stan!" I admonished, pulling myself from the door. I walked across the living room, snapped on the end table lamp that we always kept on at night then took the stairs up.

Pulling myself by the banister, the little beer buzz I had finally achieved was gone, leaving me feeling more tired than anything else. Upstairs, I stopped equidistant between David's bedroom and the room I shared with Erica. I walked over, grabbed the knob on my son's door, preparing to open it, but stopped myself. I wanted to see him, watch him sleep for a moment, kiss his forehead and wish him sweet dreams. But just like I believed Erica was doing: running her nightly schedule without me, maybe I should consider weaning myself off of my son, just in case things go the way I'm dreading they might.

I let my hand fall from the knob and went to the room across and down the hall: the home office, both Erica and I used.

I sat slumped in the chair, thinking about what Pope said earlier— that the plan Serena and I had so brilliantly pulled off, wasn't going to work.

When he had asked me for the name of the little derelict that was about to destroy my daughter's life, all I could come up with was a first name: Rasul. I dialed Serena on the phone. When she picked up, I asked: "How are things over there? Is Janis okay?"

"Everything is quiet. And your daughter is fine. The boy hasn't come back, hasn't called her—nothing. I think what we did actually worked."

"I'm hoping you're right."

"What do you mean, hoping?" Serena said.

"I need Rasul's full name. Know it?"

"Rasul Washington. Why?"

"No reason." I didn't want to worry her…at least not yet.

"Why, Stan?"

"Just tell her," Pope mouthed from his chair, listening to the conversation.

"Pope has a cop friend. He thinks we should check this boy out, make sure he's not the thug he might be pretending to be."

"Okay," Serena said, sounding worry. "That's a good idea."

"Don't worry. Everything will be fine. Relax and get some sleep."

In the office, I didn't bother even turning on a lamp, just nudged the computer mouse across the surface of the desk, awakening the Mac. It splashed me with bright, artificial light making me squint. I knew Pope's cop friend would do the job Pope he said he would, but I was anxious to get some insight on this boy: see what I could dig up. I clicked on a search engine and waited for the Google page to pop up. I was about to type in Rasul's name, when I stopped and dragged the pointer up toward the top of the screen, letting it land on HISTORY.

I stared at the word for a long moment, my finger on the clicker, afraid of what I might uncover: what sites Erica might've visited, possibly giving me insight into what was going on with her and Michael.

I'm not a snooper. I believe if you go in search of shit, you'll step right into a heaping, smoldering pile of it. But this one time my curiosity got the best of me. Clicking the button, a list of internet addresses dropped down. At that top of them was Craigslist. I clicked on it and the site filled the big desktop monitor. What I noticed first was that I wasn't looking at "Craigslist—Atlanta" but "Craigslist—Washington, D.C.".

I sat up in the chair, face nearly pressed right up on the screen, and noticed the darkened purple color—versus the blue—of the two options that had been previously searched: "HOUSING" and "FURNITURE".

I leaned away from the computer, forgetting about Rasul Washington, my mind cycling through the reasons why my wife would've been looking for housing and furniture in the city where the biological father of her son was supposed to be moving.

I couldn't answer the question, didn't want to rack my brain trying. Not tonight. But I made a note of the information I attained, clicked off the computer, and dragged myself to bed.

16

What little sleep I did get, came two hours before I was supposed to have gotten up. Rising to an empty bed, I showered, dressed and walked into a lively kitchen: sun splashing through the open blinds, NPR going on the iPod station, and David slinging Cheerios across the room from his high chair. When Erica turned around from the fruit smoothie she was blending, saw me standing there, she appeared shocked, as though I was a stranger who had crawled through the dining room window.

"Morning," she said, sounding not particularly happy to see me. "You want some of this?" she asked, pouring some of thick shake into two glasses.

"Sure," I said, taking the one she gave me, staring at her as though she was guilty of a crime.

"What?" She asked, after taking a sip of her smoothie.

"You were on Craigslist looking for housing in D.C.? Why?" I asked, not choosing to ease into the conversation, but hit her unsuspectingly in the face with it. Catch folks off guard, you get their unpolished reaction.

"You snooping, Stan? I didn't think that was you." She coolly wrapped her lips around the straw again and took another couple of pulls.

"It's not. But you were looking, right? Housing and furniture: you going somewhere?"

"Don't be ridiculous." She turned her back on me, walked across the room, bent down, retrieved errant Cheerios from the floor and tossed them in the trash, before looking back at me. "I'm helping him look for a place."

"Being his mistress wasn't enough, Erica? You have to play fucking real estate agent, too?"

"Watch your language, Stan. David is right there."

I turned, looked at the smiling boy. "Whatever. He doesn't know what the fuck I'm saying."

David giggled. "Fuh I'm sayin!" He mimicked me.

"Way to go, Stan," Erica said. "Gonna take him for a tattoo after daycare?"

"You want me to leave you, don't you?"

"No," Erica said, sounding like she actually meant that. "Why would you say that?"

"You go to the funeral when I ask you not to. You take our son, when I told you I don't want him around that man, and now this nonsense about you help him find a place to live in D.C. If you don't want me here, just tell me."

"The sooner he finds a place, the sooner he's gone. I thought that's what you wanted."

"Why would he ask for visitation rights if he's in such in a hurry to leave? Something doesn't make sense. What is he thinking?"

"I don't know what he's thinking. But you're running late," Erica said, looking over my shoulder at the wall clock.

"To hell with getting anywhere on time," I said, very seriously to Erica. "If you don't cut ties with this man, I will walk out of here."

"Will you?" She asked, staring in my eyes as though to test me, as though I was bluffing.

I glanced over at my son, who was staring back at me. I thought briefly about the life I had here, how good it's been up until only recently. Looking back at my wife, I didn't want to back-peddle from the threat I had just made, but I didn't really want to leave either.

"Look Stan, I told you there's nothing to worry about. Now we can continue discussing this nonsense, or you can take David to daycare before both you and him are late."

"We aren't done talking about this," I said, scooping David out of his chair.

"Fuh!" My son said again, giggling louder. "Fuh! Fuh! Fuck!"

Erica shook her head at me as though I was the worst fake father in the world.

17

The school day dragged and I sent three students to the principal's office for the offenses of texting in class, sniggering for no particular reason, and kicking another student's chair.

With everything going on with Erica, my bullshit tolerance meter was at zero.

After class, driving my SUV down Piedmont Road, I got my father on the phone. "Visitation rights! That's what he's trying to get, Dad?"

"Stan, I told you, he has no ground to stand on."

"Then why is he even asking? What makes him think that—"

"Stan?"

"...he can just—"

"Stan! Calm down. Calm down!" Dad yelled into the phone. "What are you doing?"

Breathing heavily, my hand clenched around the steering wheel, the cabin of my Volvo cramped, feeling like it was a thousand degrees in there, I said, "Driving."

"Then pull off the road a second before you kill yourself."

I did as asked, pulling off into a BP station, shifting the truck into Park. I tried my best to calm down, but was so wound I couldn't slow my breathing, couldn't stop myself from feeling as though I was going to explode.

"What's going on with you, son?" Dad asked. "I can hear you panting through the phone like you're digging ditches. You're gonna let this stuff kill you if you don't relax."

"Relax? Really?" I said, my voice going up octaves. "This man is gonna take my family from me! I know that doesn't mean anything to you, since you just walked away from Mom and me, but I just can't do that to my family and think it's no big deal."

There was a long pause on my father's end, then: "That's the last one I'm granting you, son. I made my mistake then, I've apologized to you for it countless times, and I'm trying to make up for it now. I love you and my grandson, and I want you two in my life. But if you can't bring yourself to forgive me, you can hang up right now, and never have to speak to me again."

"I'm sorry, Dad," I said, not needing a second to decide whether he was right in what he had said. "I'm just…" I banged the flat of my fist against the steering wheel three times. "…just…this is not going to end well. I can feel it."

"Its going to be fine, son. As an attorney, I'm telling you, legally, this man can't do a thing to you. Okay."

I took a deep breath in, exhaled, thanked my father for his reassurance, then hung up. I was about to pull back into the traffic when my cell phone rang.

"Hello," I said, seeing Serena's name on the display before answering it.

"He's taken her!" Serena said into the phone. "He came here, and they're gone!"

She was hysterical.

"What? Rasul? Was it him? He took Janis?"

I could hear the tears in her voice, the sound of her pacing quickly back and forth through the house. "Yes! Rasul busted in here, told her she was going with him."

"Did he put his hands on her? Did he force her to go?"

"When he told her about the money we gave him, she couldn't leave with him fast enough. He took our baby, Stan!" she sobbed. "He took our baby and I don't know where they could be."

"Why did you let him take her? Dammit, Serena!"

"He put a knife to my throat!"

I slammed on my brakes in the middle of afternoon traffic, horns blowing behind me. "He what?"

Sniffling, Serena said, "When I tried to pull her away from him, he grabbed a butcher's knife from the block on the counter, threw me against a wall and put it to my throat."

I could see it in my head: squat thug, his tattooed forearm braced against Serena's chest, his fist wrapped around the blade he pressed dangerously close to her throat. He violated every right she had: walked into her house, put his hands on her, then took Serena's daughter—my daughter, after taking our money.

My eyes open, I was driving again: speeding. "I'm coming there!"

"No. They're gone. You have to find her."

"Are you okay?"

"I'm fine. You have to find her," Serena said. "She's not picking up when I call her. You have to find her, Stan."

"I know, I know. I'll call her. Maybe she'll—"

"You have to find our daughter!"

"I know. She'll answer when I call. I'll bring her back. I promise."

Dialing my daughter's number, I pressed on the gas, speeding toward nowhere,

the phone ringing in my ear. "Pick up, pick up, baby! Please pick up!"

The ringing stopped. There was a click on the line, then I heard breathing.

"Baby!" I gasped. "You okay? Where are—"

"Mr. Foster...that you?" A man's voice asked.

"Who is this?" I demanded.

"You were wrong for trying to bribe me like that," Rasul said. "Especially when we told you we're in love."

"Where is she?" I yelled into the phone. "Where is my daughter?"

"I didn't mean to threaten Ms. Foster like that, but she can't stand between me and Janis. You can't; no one can. She's carrying my seed, sir."

"Goddammit! You tell me where my daughter is right now or—" I stopped, because I heard her voice in the back ground. "Janis!" I yelled into the phone, hoping she'd hear me through the mouthpiece on the other end.

"I wanna talk to him," I heard her say.

"We don't have anything to say to this man," Rasul told my daughter.

"You put her on that fucking phone, or I swear I will track you down and—"

94

"Daddy!"

The sweet sound of my daughter's voice filled my ear, calming me only the slightest bit. "Baby! Are you all right? Tell me where you are. I'm coming to get you."

"You paid him?" Janis said, not sounding in distress, as though her wrists were tied behind her back, or as though a gag had just been yanked from between her teeth. "I told you I loved him and you try to give him money to leave me? Don't you care about me?"

"I do, baby. Tell me where you are, and—"

"Don't you love me?"

"Yes! Yes!"

"Then why would you do that? Why would you want to hurt me?"

"Baby please, just listen to me," I said, my hand trembling around the phone, as I had to swerve hard to the right to avoid a car that had suddenly stopped in front of me. "Just tell me where you are, and –"

"No Dad. Maybe I'll call you later."

"But you have no place to live. Where will you go?"

"Wherever we can for five thousand dollars. Goodbye, Dad."

"No. No!" I said, pulling the phone from my ear only to see that she had hung up.

18

"What do we do?" Serena said, looking up at me from the kitchen table. Her eyes were pink and puffy, as was her nose; a wad of Kleenex was bawled up in her fist.

"Janis said she'd call me back. I believe her," I said, pacing the floor.

"We should call the police."

"Tell them what? That our daughter willfully left with her knife-wielding boyfriend after we paid him five grand to leave her alone."

"Yeah, that he put a knife to my neck," Serena said, standing from her chair, blocking the line I was pacing. "Does it even matter to you that some man was in this house and threatened to cut my throat?"

"Of course it matters. And I told you, I'll make sure we get Janis back." I glanced at my watch. "But it's late. I need to be—"

Serena grabbed my arm. "Stay. I'm scared that he'll come back."

"Serena..." I said, giving the slightest bit of thought to what she had asked, knowing Erica was waiting for me at home, but possibly not caring whether or not I returned.

"Your wife wouldn't mind," Serena said, reading my thoughts.

"What are you talking about?"

"You have to know that she doesn't love you like that."

I pulled away from Serena. "I'll find Janis," I said, choosing not to comment on Serena's opinion of my wife. "The minute I do, I'll bring her home."

I walked in the house at some time close to eight o'clock. Erica was curled up in a small blanket on the living room sofa, watching TV. When I closed the door, she didn't turn to acknowledge me.

Coming up behind her, I leaned over her shoulder, kissed the side of her neck. "Hey babe," I said.

"Hey," she said, still not taking her eyes away from the TV, still acting as though I was not there.

"You put David down already?"

As though I had said something to offend her, she finally looked at me, but only after grabbing the remote from the coffee table and muting the TV volume. "It's 9 o'clock. What do you think?"

Yeah, she normally put him down around 7:30, but that was no need to get snippy. "Is there a problem? Other than the ones Michael is causing?"

"What's going on with you and your ex-wife?"

"What? Nothing?" I said, wondering if Erica knew I had just come from there. But even if somehow she had, I'd done nothing wrong. "Nothing's going on."

"Then why did she come over here this morning before I went to work?" Erica turned the TV entirely off, as though she wanted no distractions when I gave her the explanation.

"Serena?"

"Yes, Serena. Why was she at that door?" Erica said, standing from the sofa, walking around it toward me. "And when I told her that you had already gone to work, she said that was fine, because it was me she wanted to talk to."

"You? About what?" I said, still not believing any of this.

"That I was mistreating you. That you shouldn't have to put up with the games that I'm playing."

Shaking my head, I said, "I'm sorry. Look, I had—"

"No! There's more. She walked up on me, stuck her finger in my face, said that you deserved better, but since you were so in love with me, you were too stupid to leave. And then she threatened me, said that if you came to her complaining, or depressed, or sad again about that situation with the man I fucked around on you with, then I'd be hearing from her."

Erica stared at me appearing the slightest bit shook by what Serena had supposedly told her. She had reason to be. If Erica was the prissy, cute girl in high school: Serena was the hood, street girl. Not to say that Serena was ghetto, but just two months ago, I had to drag her out of a grocery store brawl with a middle aged woman who had jumped in front of Serena in the self-checkout line. I hadn't realized that my ex-wife still had strands of the woman's weave in her fist until we got to the car.

"Are you seeing her, Stan?" Erica asked.

"What do you mean, 'seeing her'?"

"Don't play dumb with me. Are you fucking your ex-wife?"

I couldn't believe what I was hearing. Shaking my head, waving a finger in front of Erica's face, I said, "Hold it! I know, I just know *you* aren't asking *me*—"

"Just answer the fucking question, Stan." I could almost see the jealous rage boiling in her.

"No. No, okay. I'm not seeing her. We're doing nothing, but handling this situation with my daughter, okay," I said.

She looked less rattled, narrowing her eyes a little at me. "I'm going up stairs to shower. I didn't cook," she said, pulling herself up the stairs. "But you probably ate dinner with your ex-wife."

I watched my wife disappear onto the second floor, not knowing if I should've been humbled that Serena cared so much about me that she drove her ass over here and threatened bodily harm to my current wife, or pissed off that she was troubling an already rocky marriage. Either way, Serena would hear about this.

I walked around the couch, grabbed the remote to turn the TV off when my cell rang.

"Hello?" I said, after digging it out of my pocket.

"Got a sec, bro?" Pope said. "I spoke to my guy on the force."

I felt a twinge of anxiety crawl up the center of my spine. "Everything check out?" I asked, hoping it had, that this Rasul guy wasn't on the run after slicing his family and his dog up in little pieces and leaving them strewn across the front lawn.

"No, not really," Pope said, a seriousness in his voice I only seldom heard. "He has a pretty long sheet, my guy said. Drug possession, gang activity, robbery, breaking and entering, and what you need to be more concerned about: domestic abuse. He lived with a couple of girlfriends in the past, and…"

"And?" I said after Pope trailed off.

"And it's nothing that was ever proven, but he was under suspicion of murdering one of them."

Dizzied momentarily by the gravity of what was just told me, I fell back into the sofa cushions, staring blankly in front of me. "Why…why weren't they able to get him for murder?" I hesitated to ask.

"The old lady who supposedly had information that could convict turned up missing. They were never able to pin it on him. He's a bad one, Stan," Pope said. "I'm glad your plan to pay him off worked. Janis doesn't need to have anyone like that in her life."

"You're right," I said, nodding, not finding any benefit in telling Pope, at least not then, that Rasul had broken the rules of our little arrangement.

Pope told me if things changed at all with the situation, if Rasul decided to show his law-breaking face to us ever again, call him and he'd come running to help in any way he could.

"I already know that, Pope," I said sadly, thankful I had a friend like him to rely on. Disconnecting the call, I fell onto the sofa, leaned forward, my elbows on my knees, my hands clawing at the back of my head. I thought to call Serena, give her the news, but she already knew— first hand—the boy was dangerous. I called my daughter's phone instead.

Three times straight, Janis's phone rang then dumped my call to voicemail.

"Baby," I said on the last attempt. "I don't know what's really going on, but I'm worried...I'm dying over here, and I need to hear from you." I paused, feeling desperate. "Baby," I continued, owning all responsibility for what was happening. "However I failed you as a father, call me, tell me how to make it up to you, and I will. I will, Janis. I promise."

I clicked off the downstairs lights, took the stairs and found myself standing in the middle of my bedroom, the sound of shower water running behind the closed bathroom door.

I was anxious. I needed to find my daughter and thought several times about going out to look for her. But it wasn't as though my dog that darted out the front door; I wouldn't find her driving slowly down side streets, calling her name out the windows.

I slumped on the edge of the bed, realizing I could do no more than pray she does what she said she would and calls me back. About to stand from the bed, I caught a glimmer of light out the corner of my eye, and at the same time, felt a vibration on the surface of the bed. I turned, saw my wife's cell phone a few inches away, the screen just going dark.

I looked up at the bathroom door. Still I heard the spatter of water hitting the shower walls. Eyes back on the phone, I forced myself to remember that I am not a snooper. I've never tossed a woman's dresser drawers in search of condoms, never inspected the rim of her toilet boil for dried piss droplets that only a man could've left there, and never finger-swiped my way through my wife's phone, because I never felt the need to. But now, my heart in my throat, a cold bead of sweat racing down the side of my face, I needed to see from where that last text came.

Eyes up at the door again, my hand patting the comforter, I took hold of the phone, and was startled by the silence of the shower being cut off.

I swiped the phone. It lit up, giving me access. That meant my wife hadn't locked it, which meant she had nothing to hide, which made me feel even guiltier. But I was already tumbling down the rabbit hole; there was no turning back.

The text—as I had guessed—was from Michael. Behind the bathroom door, I heard the flap of fluffy bath towel, the gush of facet water, and knew in seconds Erica would be pulling open the door.

I wasn't concerned with whatever was said in the message; I hadn't time to read it. I accessed my wife's contact information, telling myself this was how I would get to Michael. I saw his number, read it aloud quickly three times, committing it to memory. I closed the menu, pressed the button, putting the phone to sleep, lay it back on the bed, then rushed out of the bedroom, as I heard the bathroom door opening behind me.

19

In the morning, I dropped David off at daycare. Unlike the norm, I made little conversation with him on the way there and was happy he was as content with playing with a plastic dinosaur I'd given him a week ago.

Sitting in the faculty parking lot, staring at my cell phone which I set in front of me on the car's dash, I wondered had I been paying too much attention to David, and not enough to my daughter: my actual child—the one that had my blood coursing through her veins, as Serena liked to remind me. If I had been more focused on her, would we be in the situation we were in now?

I glanced at my watch, saw I had five minutes left before I needed to head into class. I picked up the phone, checked it to make sure that it was on. "C'mon, Janis. Give your old man a call like you said you would. Just ring the phone," I said, focusing deeply on the screen, as though I had the power to send her a mental message from my phone to hers.

A knock came at my window startling me so, I jumped, fumbling the phone to the floor of the car. I reached down to grab it, then saw a pudgy redhead in a worn corduroy blazer standing outside my window, pointing to his wrist watch.

"Gonna be late," the fourth grade teacher said. "No naps before class," he joked, laughed then walked on.

That moment I was alarmed again by the ringing of my phone.

"Janis!" I said, the phone pressed hard to my ear.

"Dad, I only got a second."

"Are you okay? Did he hurt you?"

"What are you talking about? Of course he didn't hurt me."

She made my asking sound ridiculous, like she wasn't dating a boy with an extensive criminal background, a boy that may have murdered not one, but two people.

"Janis, do you know who you're dealing with? Do you know the kind of boy this Rasul is?"

"I didn't call to hear you tear him down. If that's what you want to do then maybe I should just hang—"

"No, no, no! I'm sorry. I'm sorry. You can talk to me, say whatever you want to say and I'll listen."

After a brief pause, Janis said, "I'm sorry about what happened yesterday. He shouldn't have done that to Mom, and he feels really bad about it."

"Okay," I said, wanting to say much more, but holding my tongue.

"And I'm sorry about being mean to you, and not calling you back. It's just you guys giving him money to—"

"I know, I know, honey. That was wrong. But your Mom is worried about you, and so am I. So why don't you just tell me where you are, so that I can come and get you."

"I..." Janis said, as though considering it. "No, I don't think that's a good idea."

"Look, baby. Whatever you want to do going forward: have the baby or whatever, we'll let you do, but you need to come home. You need to be where we know you'll be safe."

Another long pause, then: "Hold on a sec, Dad."

I heard noise: her walking across the floor, then maybe the sound of her poking fingers between window blinds, peeking out of them. She came back on, her words hurried. "I gotta go, Dad."

"Hold it! Tell me where you are."

"He's coming back. I gotta go!" she said, not sounding frightened, only anxious as if she didn't want Rasul to know she was talking to me.

"Promise you'll call me back today. I need to see you, Janis."

"Yeah, bye." The call was disconnected.

At lunchtime, I pushed open Principal Ann's office door after she invited me in. Chewing, and holding half of a bologna sandwich, she gestured to the chair in front of her desk, telling me to have a seat.

"Sorry to bother you during lunch," I said, sitting.

Principal Ann sipped from a small cardboard carton of school provided white milk, washing down the sandwich. "No, not at all. How are you, Stan?"

She hadn't realized how loaded a question that was. After hearing from Janis this morning, I was barely able to function, for it seemed every second of the morning I was pulling my cell phone from my pocket, checking it, making sure it hadn't rung. I was of little to no use to my students, who would every now and again raise a hand and ask, "Mr. Foster, are you okay?" I would smile uncomfortably, realizing I was standing frozen, midway through a sentence I had scribbled on the chalkboard.

Looking up at the principle, the older woman I'd known for several years, a woman that always treated me fairly and cared for me more like family than just faculty, I said, "To be honest, I'm not very good." I gave her a very general description of what was going on, but enough detail to see the compassionate reaction she displayed while listening. "I can finish out the afternoon, but I think I'm going to need a few days, like the rest of the week to take care of this. Is that possible?"

Nodding her head slowly, appearing as concerned as if it was her child caught up in the mess and not mine, Ann said, "I'm so very sorry. Take whatever time you need, Stan."

After class I stood in the parking lot of Starbucks off Peachtree, drinking a black coffee, my phone vibrating in my fist. The display read JANIS.

"Hello!" I answered, expecting to hear her screaming on the other end, Rasul yelling in the background, over the racket of splintering furniture and shattering glass.

"How was class, Dad?"

My heart slowed from a sprint to a trot when I heard her casual tone. "Awful. Couldn't stop worrying about you. You okay?"

"Ugh! Dad, I'm grown, all right. I'm not your little girl anymore."

"Don't say that. I told you never to say that. You'll always be my little girl," I said, smiling a little, this feeling more like the time before the introduction of the monster Rasul into my daughter's life. "Did you speak to your mother?"

"Not yet. Not really in the mood to be cursed out, you know."

"Then we'll face her together, and I'll protect you. Tell me where you are."

"No, Dad. After what you and Mom did, going behind my back."

"I'm sorry. We're sorry. We were wrong, but we only did it because we love you. Don't continue to run from us like this. If you could only know how broken up your mother is about not seeing you, about you being dragged out of her house like that. At least let me visit you. You don't have to leave with me. Just let me lay eyes on you so I can tell her you're fine."

There was a moment of silence, and I know that was my daughter weighing the pros and cons regarding the decision she was about to make. I just wished she had given as much thought to dating Rasul.

"Fine. We're in a house in Riverdale: some guy he knows."

"Is Rasul there?" I asked, needing to know what I would be facing.

"No. He's out doing the right thing, Dad; he's looking for a job." She paused, I believed waiting for me to applaud the boy's effort to get what he should've already had.

"Okay," I said, ignoring her comment. "Give me the address. I'm coming right over."

I had sped over there, weaving in and out between slower moving cars on I-85, knowing I wasn't just going there to see my daughter, have a conversation with her, but to drag her away from there as Rasul had taken her from Serena's home.

The neighborhood was as I expected: hood! There were just as many abandoned houses and homes in disrepair as there were houses that looked inhabitable.

Stepping out of my truck, I hurried up a path littered with convenience store trash: empty bags of Flamin' Hot Cheetos, Swisher Sweet wrappers and crushed cans of malt liquor. Taking the stairs two at a time, I pounded on the door after seeing only twisted wires snaking out a hole where a doorbell should've been.

Janis answered a moment later, her hair frazzled and pulled back in the typical ball. She wore sweatpants, a t-shirt and low top All-stars: what I assumed she was wearing yesterday when she was kidnapped.

"Dad, why you banging on the door like it's an FBI raid," she said, holding the door open, actually giving me a smile.

Without taking a moment to reconsider my actions, I did something I told myself I never would; I put my hands on my daughter and grabbed her tight by both arms, manhandled her, pulling her into me and dragging her out the door.

"Dad!" she cried, whirling about, staring at me like I might have not been her father, but some man impersonating him. "What are you doing? Let me go!" She tried to fight me, pry my hands loose.

I dragged her down the half dozen stairs, started pulling her down the walk, fighting off her efforts to break free, while drawing the attention of an old lady sitting on her porch across the street. Alarmed, she stood, shuffled as quickly as her body would allow into the house. To do what: call the police, or tell her out-of-work, adult son, Trey, a girl is being raped? Or maybe to grab a shotgun? Neither scenario I needed, so at the door of my truck, I pressed Janis's back to it, grabbed her firmly by the cheeks as I saw her mother do countless times, squeezed, and said, "Janis, I'm sorry this is happening, but if you don't shut up and get your little ass in the truck this very minute, I swear, I'll forget the fact that you're my daughter."

Seeing the fear in her eyes, I did not have to wonder if she would comply. I opened the passenger door, and she obediently climbed in. I shut it, hurried around the truck, hopping in, at the same time seeing a large, shirtless man—one half of his hair braided, the other in a half afro—hurrying out the house, both him and the old lady climbing down the stairs as I sped away.

20

At the open front door of her house, Serena threw her arms around Janis as though I had just rescued her from Al-Qaeda militants.

"Thank God! Thank God!" Serena said, her face buried in Janis's shoulder, my daughter's arms hanging at her sides. She held Janis, looked her over. "Are you okay?"

"Why wouldn't I be?" Janis said, attitudinal, not appreciating the way I nabbed her. She let me know that the entire way home.

"I asked you a question," Serena said, her voice now more firm than thankful.

"I'm fine," Janis grunted.

"Then get in that house right now!" Serena said.

The girl grunted again, shot daggers at me over her shoulder, lowered her head and stomped inside.

"Where did you find her?" Serena asked me.

"Riverdale...some house."

"Was Rasul there?" she asked.

"No. Supposedly out looking for a job."

"Yeah, right."

"What are you going to do with Janis?"

"First, I'm taking the child's cell phone, then I'm locking her ass in her room for ten years."

"The boy might come here. If he does, don't let him in, and call me right away. I'll be here in minutes. Okay."

Serena stared at me. "If you're so worried about him coming back, you should just stay?"

"I already told you I can't. And after what you did, I shouldn't even be here."

"The wife told you about my visit, huh," Serena said, half smiling.

"Yes she did."

"I'm sorry, but you know I—"

"Don't," I said, raising a finger, hoping to silence her. She took my hand. I didn't pull away. She kissed the tip of my finger.

"You deserve better, but if you're cool over there, then I can't be happier for you," she lied.

The conversation Serena had with my wife yesterday, and Erica's disapproval of that meeting was only half the reason I left Serena's. With Janis so much on my mind this morning, I walked out of the house, forgetting the scrap of paper with Michael's phone number on it.

Although I didn't read the text he sent my wife last night, I wasn't overlooking the fact that he had the fucking balls to have texted her, which meant they were communicating on a regular basis: something I could no longer tolerate. I needed to put an end to that pronto. I needed to get a hold of him.

A block from my house, I slammed on the brakes, halting the truck in the middle of the street. I looked into the rearview mirror, setting eyes on the car that was just a blur a second ago as I drove by it. I threw the truck in reverse, rolled back, stopping alongside Michael's Infiniti, or at least what I thought was his car. I shifted the Volvo in park, left it sitting in the middle of the street as I got out and examined the car. Walking around it, there was nothing to distinguish it from any other Infiniti G35. I didn't know his plate number, didn't see any mail on the dash with his name on it, or anything else that would let me know this car was his. Hoping the man wasn't foolish enough to walk into my home again, I climbed back into my truck, continued up the block to my house, telling myself either Michael had a friend who lived in our neighborhood, or that very moment, he was at my house, and didn't want anyone to know.

21

I stood in my living room after pushing open the front door, bracing myself against the horrible scene I had discovered on two previous occasions: one nearly three years ago when my wife told me she was pregnant, and just days ago, when she told me Michael's family had been incinerated in their beds. But this time, no one was in my living room. I turned in a half circle, looked around, thought of calling out for my wife, but stopped myself. If there was a chance she was here with that man, I needed to catch them in the act. Maybe then, I could accept that trying to save my family was no longer worth my time.

I took the stairs up, and on the second floor, I forced myself to believe she simply would not do that to me. After all we've been through, the love I believe we still shared, the warnings I gave her—she would not be so foolish as to do what I feared most.

I looked down the hall to our bedroom door, saw that it was closed, when normally it would've been open. I shut my eyes against images like the ones from that dream trying to get into my brain: my wife's sweat covered back, her hips and ass flared out over Michael's spread thighs, one hand reaching behind her, grabbing him between the legs, both of them crying out in unspeakable pleasure.

I started down the hall, now fueled with a passion to the do the man harm if what I had just envisioned was actually happening. But halfway down the hallway, I was stopped, as though hitting an invisible wall. I stood in front of David's open bedroom door, my mouth falling open, unable to comprehend what I saw: Erica facing my son's window, her back to me, Michael standing beside her. He was not naked, but in slacks, shirt and tie, his jacket, folded and set down on my son's bed. Erica was rubbing a hand over his back: a gentle, slow, caring motion, as though she loved him.

I felt myself take two slow steps back, bumping into the wall behind me, shocked that they had not seen me or felt my presence—my stare burning through them. But the two of them there was not what made me want to slide down the wall, fall to my knees and sob. In Michael's arms was my son. David's arm was looped around the man's neck, his little chin hooked over Michael's shoulder.

A quick note about my son: there have been occasions when I walked into his room at night to tuck him in, and upon entering, I was startled to see him staring wide-eyed up at me. Startled by the scene that could've come from any horror movie, I laughed and asked him what he was doing awake. He continued to stare at me, his face pressed against his pillow, his little body not moving at all under his blanket. Calling his name, worried, I asked if he had heard me. When he didn't respond, I was down, kneeling at his bedside, my face very close to his. That was when I heard him lightly snoring. It happened several times after that: while I drove, David strapped into his car seat, or while watching cartoons beside me on the living room sofa, I would look up to see his eyes open, unblinking, staring right at me as he slept like a rock. It was so unsettling that all I could do was laugh to myself.

But now, standing in the hallway, staring at my son, resting on his biological father's shoulder, his eyes were open, staring back at me. My heart broke because I didn't know if he was sleeping again, or if he was wide awake, so content with the man, that he made no moves to push away from him even though the only man he knew as his father was standing in front of him.

I pushed up off the wall; it took every ounce of the strength I had.

Erica's head was now on Michael's other shoulder, a hand on David's back, both her and Michael staring out the window, like the close knit, loving family, she had promised we'd be.

I thought to go in there, destroy the fantasy they were living: yell at my wife, threaten the man, grab one of David's arms, wage a tug of war with Michael, my child screaming between the two of us. But what good would come from that? I would only hurt my child. I turned, walked down the hallway, down the stairs and out the front door.

I slammed myself inside my truck, yelled at the top of my lungs, beat my fists against the steering wheel, the dash, the doors: against any surface that would cause me pain when I struck it. Breathing hard, my chest heaving, I stared into my thoughts, smeared the tears away from my eyes. I thought about that man holding my son, my wife stroking his back, the three of them in my house as though it was he who belonged there and not I.

I found my hand on the truck door handle, about to push it open to go back inside, end this thing once and for all. I couldn't do it, knowing if I were to force Erica to get rid of Michael, she would most likely take David with her, and I wouldn't be able to bare that. My son needed me. I won't just walk away from him like my father did me, or let her drive me away, as I allowed Serena to force me away from Janis.

I pulled my hand from the door. I needed to think this situation through. Like Pope said, I needed to confront Michael: have a man to man with him. If things were brought to him the right way, he'd understand. Maybe he'd just leave my family alone.

His number was in the house, in the pocket of the pants I was wearing last night. Knowing it was there was a comfort. Tomorrow I'd call him.

I slipped the key in the ignition, about to start it up when my cell phone rang, Serena's name flashing on the screen. I felt a tinge of anxiety, hoping Rasul was not crazy enough to show back up at her house, but when I answered the call, I heard Serena crying and Rasul yelling.

22

Fifteen minutes later, I ran from my car up the path to the house; the door was wide open. Again, I heard Rasul's crazed yelling. It hit me on the street the moment I threw open the SUV door.

Inside was torn up worse than it was before: chairs knocked over, sofa legs turned upward and pictures yanked from the walls. When I stepped in, I saw Serena cowering in a corner of the living room. Rasul was beside the fireplace, both hands on a corner of the wall mounted, 50-inch flat screen TV.

"Tell me where the fuck she's at?" He yelled at Serena unaware of me, until I yelled his name. Rasul turned, his eyes bugging in his head. He looked manic, like he hadn't slept in days, like he was on the ragged edge and common sense had nothing to do with what he was doing—or what he would do. The boy brushed at his nose, sniffing hard.

"Where is Janis, Mr. Foster? You took her from me. Where the fuck she at?" He yelled, swiping at his nose and sniffing again.

I shot a questioning glance at Serena.

"She's not here," she cried back. "Really. She left and went—"

"No!" I said, raising both hands, not needing Rasul to know. "It doesn't matter where she went."

"It fucking does matter where she went!" Rasul yelled, pulling on the corner of the flat screen, yanking it down from over the mantle, where it fell onto the brick fireplace landing, the screen cracking.

"Rasul, calm down," I said, hands still up, approaching him like one would a rabid, slobbering dog.

"I don't need to do nothing!" More sniveling: eyes darting all about the room, as if he expected Janis to crawl out from under one of the sofa cushions that had been knocked to the floor.

"You take something, Rasul? You on something?" I said, knowing someone revved up on drugs when I see them.

"No!" He snapped. Then... "Don't matter if I had. I need to know where Janis is, and I need to know now!" He set his eyes on Serena.

"Rasul! No! Look over here. Keep your eyes on me."

Only ten feet separating them, he took a step toward her. "You took my woman. What if I were to take yours," he said to me, continuing to walk slowly toward her: big jeans sagging from his ass, Timberland boots stepping over the mess he created on the living room floor.

"Stan!" Serena cried, her back pressed as far into the corner as the converging walls would allow.

"Rasul!" I yelled.

Without looking back, he said, "Fuck you, Mr. Foster," and reached around himself, raised the tail of his flannel button-down and grabbed the handgun that appeared in the small of his back. He pulled it, four feet away from Serena, pointed it in her direction, but by that time, the momentum of a speeding freight train was already behind me. I had leapt from my feet, throwing myself into him. We fell to the floor, my body on top of his, the gun jumping from his grasp, tumbling across the carpet toward the fireplace.

Serena's screams in my ears, and in my eyes, the dark blur of Rasul's beard, the white smear of his eyes, his teeth exposed from the snarl of his lips, we wrestled: arms and legs locking, rolling over each other, desperately trying to free a fist or a foot to use as a weapon on the other. He was successful: struck me across the jaw with a punch I didn't see, knocking me off of him. On my back, I saw him scurrying across the carpet on his hands and knees. Serena screamed that he was going for the gun.

I flipped over, half crawled and leapt toward him, saw him as he reached out, wrapped his fist around the weapon, turned and started to point it at me. I was on him, grabbed his wrist with both my hands. On top of him, I bang his hand down on the brick landing of the fireplace. He cried out, dropped the gun. He punched me again in the face. I was dazed, thought for a moment I'd pass out, but felt his hands reach up and lock around my throat.

Grunting and cursing, I heard him say, "I'll kill you, Mr. Foster! I'll kill your motherfucking ass!"

And he was really trying to do that. I felt myself becoming light headed as I reached down, found his neck, clamped my hands around it. I felt Serena's hands on my shoulders, as if trying to rescue me, rip me from Rasul's grip. I knew he wouldn't let go until I was dead...or he was.

The room spinning, the light dimming around me, Serena's voice growing distant, I knew I would pass out any moment if I didn't do something to save myself. With the last bit of my strength, I tightened my grip around Rasul, raised his head, his neck and shoulders following, and with all my weight, slammed his skull back onto the floor. There was a deafening "crack": the sound of a thick branch snapping in half, then Rasul's hands fell away from me. Dazed and coughing, I fell on him, my face dropping beside his, my nose pressing against the floor, the blood that leaked from his broken skull, across the brick fireplace landing, painted my cheek as I gasped for air.

Serena was pulling me by the arm. I rolled off Rasul and hadn't known till Serena had me standing—my arm around her shoulder, hers around my waist—that he was dead.

Rasul lay on his back, arms spread perpendicular to his body, jeans low to expose multicolored boxers. He stared up at Serena and I through lifeless eyes, the dark red blood creeping slowly across the bricks of the fireplace landing.

"We...we..." I said trembling. "We have to call the police. We have to—"

Serena spun me to face her. "No, Stan. We aren't calling anyone."

"But he's dead," I said, taking my eyes from hers, looking back at the body. "I killed him and—"

She took my cheeks in her hands, wrenched my face back to hers. "Yes you killed him, because he was trying to kill you. I don't need the police finding someway to change that and you land in jail for life for killing some thug."

"Then what do we do?"

Serena looked over at Rasul, no sympathy or compassion on her face. "We get rid of the body."

23

It was dark, the sky overhead filled with stars. Pope and I had driven an hour south into a rural part of Georgia: lots of grass, trees and empty spaces: no people or much of anything else around for miles. I sat on the tailgate of his pickup truck, feeling traumatized after committing the murder.

When I realized Serena was right about needing to get rid of Rasul's body, we were faced with the question of just how we'd do that and where we'd dump it. I didn't think Serena was strong enough to help me lift the dead weight, so that was another problem.

Knowing the honest man Pope was, when I told Serena there was no one else I could call for help, she questioned whether or not he could be trusted not to expose us, and if he'd be willing to go along. The phone to my ear, I told her we had no other choice but to find out.

He came quickly, rolled up behind the house, not in his Camaro, but in his pickup truck. After I let him in, he saw Serena standing in a corner of the kitchen, her arms hugging herself. He asked her if she was okay. She nodded. Pope gave her a hug and told her not to worry, that everything was going to work out just fine.

In the living room, we stood over Rasul's body, Pope looking down on it, telling me he had a tarp on the truck and he'd be back in a minute.

Now, we sat on the pickup's tailgate, passing a fifth of Jack Daniels back and fourth. I held it, my hand trembling around the neck, as I stared down at the three foot, circular hole we had finished digging not long ago. I attempted to pass the bottle back to Pope.

He shook his head. "Nah, hit it again. You need it."

I did as instructed, wincing against the strength of the liquor.

"He was in Serena's house, Stan. You said he was going after her with a gun. We know what his record looked like. You had no choice," Pope said, trying again to convince me that the killing was justified.

After leaving the house and driving for an hour, landing in a densely wooded area, we dragged the body from the truck, then dug the six foot deep ditch.

"So we just drop him in and throw dirt on him?" I asked, holding one of the two shovels Pope had brought.

"Yeah, but first we have to make sure if someone finds him, they won't be able to identify him by his fingerprints or dental records."

"How do we do that?"

Pope walked to the truck, came back with an ax. "We have to take off his hands and his head."

I couldn't watch as Pope swung the ax as though chopping wood. Three swifts swings and the identifiable parts were separated. We buried the body, then drove another fifteen minutes to the spot where were now. I took another swig of the liquor, shifted my eyes from the hole to the plastic Walmart bag that lay beside it. Inside were the hands and the head; the ties of the bag double knotted, sticking up like bunny ears.

126

"You wanna do the honors?" Pope asked, as though none of this fazed him. I didn't know if it had something to do with the four years he spent over in Saudi as an Army machine gunner, but I could only assume it had.

"No. Why don't you?"

He hunched his shoulders, walked over to the bag, and as though putting a golf ball inches from the hole, with the side of his boot, he shoved the bag into the ditch we had dug. I watched him refill the hole, pack the dirt tight with the back of the shovel. He walked back over, tossed the shovels in the pickup, then the ax, after wiping the blood off the blade with a rag and ammonia he poured from a small bottle.

"Stan!" Pope said, as though he had called my name more than once and I hadn't heard him.

"Yeah," I said, turning to him.

He smiled, dropped heavy hands on either of my shoulders. "Janis is your baby girl. That man in the dirt was trying to hurt her, trying to take her away from you. I told you what I'd do to someone if they tried to mess with my girls like that, right?"

I nodded.

"You did the right thing: the only thing. You manned the fuck up and handled your business. Nothing to second-guess, nothing to let haunt you. You did what had to be done to protect the ones you love. You with me?"

I nodded again.

"No. I need to hear you say it."

I stared at him uncertain. He stared right back as though trying to transfer his strength. "What do you want me to say again?"

"That you did this to protect the ones you love, and you're not wrong for doing that."

"I killed Rasul to protect the ones I love, and I'm not wrong for having done it. That okay?" I asked, timidly.

Pope smiled wider, slapped me hard on the side of the shoulder, nearly knocking me off the tailgate. "Perfect, Stan!"

We climbed into the cab, Pope sticking the key into the ignition, ready to fire up the engine. Before he did, he turned to me. "Regarding the other thing...you know...with that Michael character. Don't kill him or anything," Pope smiled a little. "But he's threatening your family too, so, he needs to be dealt with as well. Got that?"

I slumped in my seat, my chin falling to my chest, still messed up about the murder I had committed, but not losing sight of the business I still had to handle with Michael. "Yeah," I said, more to myself than to Pope. "I got it."

24

I watched the brake lights on Pope's truck brighten as he stopped at the stop sign then disappeared around the corner after dropping me off in front of Serena's. I wasn't sure if I'd ever be able to thank the man for what he had just done, but what I did know was that I might've been sitting in a jail cell by now if it wasn't for him.

Inside, the house was clean and reordered as much as it could've been. The broken flat screen TV was propped against the fireplace, the pictures had been removed, probably taken out to the garage. The glass was swept up, and everything was put back in its place.

When I walked into the kitchen, Serena was there, watching the counter TV on mute from a seat at the table, a steaming cup of tea cradled in her hands. She saw me, set the cup down, hurried over and threw her arms around me, burying her face into my shoulder as if she wished to forget what had happened.

I held her for a moment then leaned away, asking: "Did Janis make it back?"

"Yeah. Came in asking questions about the TV. I told her I tried adjusting it on the wall and it fell and broke. She seemed to have believed it."

"Good," I said.

"What happened with…" Serena asked, walking back to her chair, but not sitting.

I nodded, feeling unable to speak about it. "It's…it's done." She walked back over, touched my face.

"We did this for our daughter. We're gonna be fine. Be strong, okay."

I nodded again, blinking quickly, for some reason feeling sorry for the kid, remembering the flash of his open eyes staring at me as Pope shoved his severed head into the Walmart bag. "Yeah, I know," I said, trying to believe what she had said.

She forced a reassuring smile, walked to one of the kitchen drawers, then before pulling it open, looked past me toward the door to make sure we were alone. She took something out, kept it hidden with her hand until she set it on the kitchen table. It was a cell phone.

"Rasul's," Serena said. "Found it on the floor after you all took him. Janis has been texting him, asking where he's been."

Of course she was, I thought, taking a seat in front of it, staring hatefully at it like it was a living, breathing extension of him. "And?"

"And I've been answering back like I was Rasul: told her that the two of them need to take a break for a couple of days while her father cooled down."

"That should work for a little while," I said.

"Then what?"

"I don't know," I said.

It was after 11 o'clock when I walked into the kitchen of my own home, saw my wife stand from the table. She was drinking wine from a stemmed glass. She took one step forward then stopped. "Where have you been? I've called you."

Actually she had called twice. I saw notices in my missed calls log as Pope drove me back toward Serena's. The time stamps said the first one came in around the time Rasul was trying to kill me, the other, when I was attempting to stop myself from throwing up as Pope whacked off the boy's hands.

"Sorry," I said, trancelike. "I couldn't get away from what I was doing."

"Exactly what were you doing?" Erica said, accusingly.

I was exhausted, and I believed, still in a good deal of shock. "Nothing," I mumbled. "Just need to shower and go to bed."

She looked me up and down, shook her head then let me leave. After two steps, she said, "Hold it. Is that blood?"

I felt her tugging at the back of my shirt. I turned, snatched the tail from her grasp. "No," I said. "Now I told you I'm tired. I'm going to bed!"

Running the shower: steam still floating in the bathroom, the mirror still fogged with it, I picked up my clothes from the heap I had dropped them in. Examining them, I saw the blood Erica had spotted. It was on the back of my shirt: dime sized drops, more smeared near the left pocket of my pants. I don't know how I, Pope and Serena had missed that, but we had.

In my bathrobe and slippers, I walked past our home office—the door closed, sounds of Erica working inside—down the stairs, out the back door, and pitched the clothes in the dumpster. Afterward, I walked back up stairs, peeling off my robe and sliding into bed, thinking the garbage truck would come tomorrow and the only evidence linking me to Rasul's murder would be gone forever. In regard to the guilt I was feeling about killing the boy, I could only hope it would pass soon.

The next morning, I woke from a night of restless sleep to see Erica standing at the side of our bed, her arms crossed.

"What?" I said, raising up on my elbows.

"What were you really doing last night, Stan?"

"I…I told you nothing important."

"In your sleep you were doing a lot of thrashing about, and a lot of talking."

I bit down on a corner of my lip nearly hard enough to draw blood, hoping that I didn't—

"You said something about murdering—"

"I didn't."

"—murdering someone named Rasul. Isn't that the boy your daughter is having trouble with?"

"I didn't say that!" I said, sitting up.

"You did, Stan. You said it a lot. Like you almost couldn't stop. Tell me you didn't do…" she put a hand to her mouth, shock filling her eyes, as if only then she could believed I had killed the boy.

"I told you I didn't. I don't know what you're—"

"Stan, please!" she cried. "If you've done what you said, just tell me! Don't lie to me about something like that. Please!"

I sighed, falling onto my back, shut my eyes, hoping I wouldn't regret what I was about to do. "He had a gun and he was trying to shoot me. I had to defend myself. Rasul ended up dead."

She stared at me, mouth agape, eyes questioning. When I said nothing, she turned, took steps away from me, shaking her head. "And what...what happened to his body?" Erica asked, turning to face me.

"It was taken care of," I said, feeling sick to my stomach all over again. "It's best we leave it there."

"You mean you didn't call the police. You said it was self defense, that he a gun. Why not call the police. Don't you think—"

"I don't know," I said, cutting Erica off. I pushed the comforter off me and got out of bed, stood in front of her, looking in her eyes. "I did what I had to do. I'm not a murderer or anything."

"I'm not saying you are."

"Then are we okay with this?" I asked. "I'm forgetting it ever happened. Can you do the same? I mean, this won't affect how you see me, how you see me as David's father. Will it?"

"No." She shook her head almost immediately, as though certain of the answer. She stood, pressed into me, wrapping her arms around my neck. "You did it because you had to. That's what happened, right?"

"Right," I said, my arms at my sides. "If he hadn't died, I would've."

"Then this will be our secret, and like you said, we'll forget about it; it never happened."

I stood there, legs weak, still shaking after everything that had happened. I wanted nothing more than to relax in Erica's arms, accept her sympathy, but knowing just yesterday she was in the room down the hall with Michael, I could not. My forehead on her shoulder, I frowned, wanting to mention what I had saw, but my mind was still drowning in the turbulent events of last night.

"Thank you for understanding," I told Erica, easing out of her embrace.

25

That morning, despite the news I had given Erica yesterday, my wife made me and David breakfast as she always had, but when I stood preparing to take our son to school, she reached for him and said, "Don't worry about it this morning. I can take him, Stan. I'm going to work early today."

Mildly surprised, I said, "But I don't have to go to work at all. I told you I took some days off to deal with...you know."

"Then maybe that's what you should be doing," she said smiling, attempting to soften the abrasiveness of the comment. At the same time, she was hoisting David up from under his arms, out of the chair, as if to end all debate on the subject. She probably saw me as a cold-blooded killer now, even though she had said knowledge of the murder wouldn't change things. Now I felt she wanted me nowhere near her son. I let her take him, knowing there was no arguing with her at this time, and that there were still loose ends I needed to tie up regarding Rasul's death.

Standing on the front porch, watching as Erica drove off with David, I called Serena, told her I thought it was a bad idea for her to continue to text our daughter as the man I had murdered.

"We don't want a record of texts coming from our house when he wasn't there. Send Janis a final message as Rasul, telling her he doesn't have time to mess with a girl who's father was so much into her business. Let her down easy, Serena," I said. "Let her know it's not her fault, but mine. Then destroy the phone, drive down some deserted highway and toss the pieces out the window, okay."

"Yeah okay, Stan," Serena said.

Later, throughout the course of the day, I tried countless times to get in touch with Michael: pacing the living room while Erica was at work, from the seat of my parked truck, or standing in line at the liquor store. The phone would ring several times then go to voicemail and I would cringe at the sound of his deep, charismatic voice, imagine him using that same tone to whisper in my wife's ear, tell her things that would make her smile. I disconnected the call each time, not wanting to leave a message, alerting him to the fact that I was onto him, that I had gotten his number. I trusted that next time he'd pick up and we'd have our much-needed discussion.

The next morning after I confessed to my wife that I had killed Rasul, I woke up in bed alone. That was nothing very new, but sitting up, looking around the sunlit room, I had gotten the feeling that she had never come to bed. Examining her side, it appeared, for the most part, still made up, as though it had never been slept in. After showering and dressing, I went downstairs to ask her about that, but found that she had left. It was a full hour before I would've normally taken David to school, and standing there in the quiet kitchen alone, I wondered if my wife was now so frightened that she could not sleep in the same bed, or even sit at the table and have breakfast with me.

26

Later that afternoon, I received a call from a Serena telling me that our daughter was having a hard time with the text message that was sent to her from Rasul.

"She said she doesn't believe he'd just leave her like that. That he'd just up and disappear," Serena told me. "She'd already been back to the friend's house where they stayed, and the guy told Janis the last place Rasul said he was going was to get her."

"And now she's thinking—"

"We had something to do with him leaving her. She's not believing a word when I tell her otherwise. I need you to sit down and talk to her."

"Okay, fine," I said, my stress building, having to deal with Erica and the games she was playing with David, my failed attempts to get a hold of Michael, and the gnawing guilt I was still feeling for having to put down Rasul. "I'll call her to have lunch or something."

That night, Erica and I ate dinner in near complete silence, our heads down, quickly looking away on the two occasions our eyes accidently met. Finishing, I took our plates, rinsed them, set them in the dishwasher then said I was going up to check on David.

"I'll come with you," she said, starting to rise from her seat a little too quickly.

"That's okay. Honestly, I'd really rather spend a little time alone with him. For some reason, I feel I haven't had the chance to do that lately."

Up out of her chair and out from around the table, Erica said, "And I'd really rather go with you."

She walked behind me up the stairs, but he didn't come in the room, just stood in the doorway, keeping an eye on me as though I were a convicted child molester. Afterward, walking down the hall together, she stopped at the guest bedroom door.

"What are you doing?" I asked.

Her hand on the doorknob, having pushed it open a bit, she said, "I'm sleeping in here tonight." There was an apology in her tone, as though that made a difference.

"You slept in there last night, too, didn't you?"

Erica nodded.

"Why?"

"You know the mattress in here is firmer," she said, rubbing the small of her back, adding theatrics to the lie. "I must've twisted it somewhere. The harder bed helps."

I stared at her in disbelief. "This has nothing to do with what I did: what I had to do?"

She gave me a condescending smile and rubbed her back again. "No. It's just what I said. Goodnight, Stan." She pushed through the door and closed it.

The next day, I walked through a restaurant of miss-matched tables and chairs, and graffiti-stained walls, peopled with mid-town hippy-types. Fellini's Pizza on Ponce was where Janis and I agreed to meet. Janis was already there, sitting in a booth. By the bags under her eyes she looked as though she had been pulling all-nighters since the news that Rasul had dumped her.

I leaned in to kiss her cheek; she didn't reach to meet me as she normally did, just sat back and accepted the greeting as though she could've just as easily done without it. I sat.

"What do you want to eat?" I asked, sitting on the opposite side of the booth.

"Nothing. I can't eat," she mumbled. "I've been texting Rasul like a million times a day," she said, producing her phone, staring at it, as if hoping this would be the moment he finally responded. "I even called him. Nothing."

"Why would he text you back, Janis? Your mother said he ended things."

"I don't believe that. I'm having his baby. She's lying."

"Why would she do that?"

"The same reason the two of you would fucking give him five thousand dollars to leave me!" She said, catching the attention of a couple of tattooed diners, dousing their peperoni slices with hot sauce. I thought about telling her to watch her language, but we were long past that.

"Did you do something to him, Dad?"

139

I remained calm, gave her the practiced look of innocence, knowing she would accuse me of something. "Like what, Janis? Don't be ridiculous."

"I don't know. Give him another five thousand," she said grasping, trying to find any other reason for him not wanting to be with her. "Because…" her voice cracked, then she shut her eyes as though about to cry. I was up out of my side of the booth and into hers, my arm around her. Pulling her in, kissing her forehead, I said, "I'm so sorry, baby. But if he doesn't want to be with you, there's nothing we can do to make him."

She pushed away from me, sniffling. "Promise me you did nothing to him. Promise and hope to die that you did nothing to make him leave me."

"I promise and hope to die I had nothing to do with him leaving, Janis," I said, not liking the idea of lying to my daughter, but told myself it was for the greater good.

After driving Janis home, I walked around the truck, opened the door for her and gave her a hug. Not letting her go, I said, "You know everything's going to be all right, don't you."

She nodded, pulled away, stared at me a moment, as though still having doubts about what I said back at the pizza place, but didn't care to talk anymore about it. "Goodbye Dad. I love you."

"And that's all that matters," I said, releasing her from our hug, but holding onto her hand. "Now that he's gone, I want us to get back to focusing on you. We need to get you back in school, and a decision will have to be made about…" I glanced down at her stomach, insinuating the baby.

"Dad, really? I mean, really?" she said, not appreciating being pushed to make such major decisions. "I know there are things I need to think about, but Rasul just dumped me. One thing at a time. Please."

"Okay. You're right." I pulled her back to me, kissed her on the cheek. "We'll talk about it all next week."

Inside the Volvo, I watched as my daughter disappeared behind the front door of the house. I started the truck, let the engine run, while I pulled out my cell phone attempting to reach Michael. I started to dial his number when my phone chirped with an incoming text message. I smiled, thinking the text would be from Serena, thanking me for the talk I had with our daughter. I opened the message, saw that it came from a blocked number, then read words that had me whirling around, checking the back seat to ensure I was alone in the truck. Shaken, I looked out all the windows, eyed the sidewalks up and the down the street, then turned back to the message on my phone to read again the words I could not believe:

I KNOW YOU MURDERED RASUL

27

"This shit is not funny!" I told Pope when he picked up his phone.

"Dude, calm down. Exactly what shit are you talking about?"

"The text you just sent me." There were two more after the first.

THE SENTENCE FOR FIRST DEGREE MURDER IS 20 YEARS

Then:

I HOPE YOU ENJOY GETTING FUCK UP THE ASS. THAT WILL BE YOUR
LIFE

"I haven't sent you any text," Pope said. "I'm sitting here at work."

Pope could be a joker, but this was a bit harsher than I was used to him coming. Still hoping that he was lying, I said, "I don't believe you. No one else knows."

"Knows about what?"

My eyes rolling left and right, I said, "About what we did the other night."

A moment of silence, then: "Are you talking about—"

"Yes."

"Why would I—"

"You need to meet me," I said, already driving, heading in the direction of the bar where we usually drank.

"I told you I'm at work."

"Take off. Meet me at the spot in 20 minutes, Pope!" I disconnected the call and threw the phone to the passenger seat.

Exactly 20 minutes later, Pope was coming through the door: khaki pants, print tie swinging from a denim collared shirt. I half stood from the bar—a short glass of whisky in one hand—I reached out the other before he made it to me. "Give me your phone."

"I told you it wasn't me," Pope said, handing it over. I kicked back the last of what was in my glass, blindly called to the bartender to give me a refill and one for my friend, then sifted through Pope's text messages. I found nothing but stuff to and from his wife, his daughters, a couple of names I didn't know, and me: none of which had anything to do with Rasul's murder, or me rotting away in jail.

"Told you," he said beside me, eyeing the tiny screen as I continued to search for what wasn't there.

I set his phone down on the bar in front of him and not a second later, mine lit on the bar beside me, with an incoming text. I hesitated to pick it up.

"Aren't you gonna check to see what that is?" Pope asked.

"I know it's whoever it is." I grabbed the phone, set it in front of him. "You check it."

Pope picked up the phone, swiped the screen with a thumb. I watched the expression on his face darken, his brows furrow as his eyes moved over the screen.

"What?" I asked.

"Nothing. I'm going to delete it."

I snatched the phone from him before he could and read the text.

I HEARD THEY KNOCK ALL THE TEETH OUT THE MOUTHS OF SOME MEN SO THEY DON'T BITE WHEN THEY'RE FORCED TO SUCK PRISON DICK

I wanted to sling the phone across the room, shatter it into a million pieces against a wall, but what good would that do me?

Pope grabbed his drink, downed half of it. "Who knows besides Serena?"

"No one," I lied. "I couldn't have Pope going off on me because I slipped up, blabbered in my sleep what we had done. Besides, it made no sense telling him that. I really felt our secret was safe with Erica. She wouldn't tell a soul. Regardless of whatever we were going through, she wasn't evil enough to want me going to jail, which is where she had to have known I would've landed if anyone found out about this.

"You sure?" Pope asked.

"No one else knows."

Pope spun slowly on his stool, took in all the faces of the people sitting around us at the bar and in the dining area, as though the person that had texted me might've been there, wanting to see the anguish he was causing me. Turning to me, Pope said, "Obviously this person wants something. Eventually he or she will tell us, then we'll decide how to deal with."

I sat drinking with Pope for a couple of more hours, then when to a package store for a bottle. I stopped my truck under the overpass of a deserted street in Vine City. I turned my phone off, drunk till the strength of the liquor closed my eyes, then woke up, darkness around me, my head spinning, only a quarter of the bottle left, sitting between my thighs.

When I got home it was dark outside, sometime after 11 P.M. I stumbled through the front door, tripped up the stairs, stepped out of my shoes, leaving them in the middle of the floor, and dragging a hand against the hallway wall for support, I walked down to my bedroom. Inside, I was not surprised to see that the bed was still made: no sign of Erica. That was probably best; I didn't need her complaining about me walking in late drunk. I was about to undress when I decided I'd kiss my son goodnight first.

I gently pushed open his door, surprised to see that his nightlight wasn't on. I searched for it in the dark, groping the wall with my palm. Finding it, I switched the light on, it revealing that his bed was as empty and neatly made as mine. I thought for a moment, wondering where he might be.

At the guest bedroom, I grabbed the knob, but when I attempted to turn it, it would not budge. I raised a fist, about to bang on the door, when it opened. Erica stood behind it, wearing a nightgown, looking sleepy-eyed as though she was near drifting off. Behind her, the glow of the TV bathed the room in blue light.

"What are you doing?" I said, trying to look over her shoulder. She moved to her right to block me, saying, "I told you I have a bad back and—"

"And does our son have a bad back, too? Is that why he's in there?"

"Stan, I just—"

I wasn't interested in another lie. I tried to step past her, asking that she let me in. Again, she moved in front of me.

"Let me in!" I said, pressing a palm into the door and forcing it open. David was in the bed, wearing his pajamas, soundly sleeping. I spun to Erica. "What is this? What are you doing? And don't you fucking say anything about you having a bad back."

After looking as though that was exactly what she was going to say, she shook her head, sighing heavily. "I'm a little afraid, Stan, all right. Do you realize what you did? You killed a man, and you expect me to just act as though nothing has happened?"

"What would you rather me have done, get killed myself? Why are you locking yourself up in this room with my son? Why are you acting as though I'm a danger to the two of you, as though you don't know who I am?"

"Sometimes I'm not sure I do anymore." The comment came from under her breath, like I wasn't supposed to hear it. "Sometimes, I think you're not the same man I married."

Those words hurt more than any she could've said, implying that she had made a mistake, that if she had all the information she would've never married me, and that very moment, she might've been considering reversing the error of her ways, which caused that image of her, Michael, and my son, hugging across the hall, to pop up in my head again.

"So what? You'd rather me be like Michael? Is that what you're saying?"

Erica threw her hands up, waved them in wild, billowy movements. "And here we go again. Every time things aren't going right between us, it's always his fault. What makes it Michael's fault this time?"

"Me walking into my house in the middle of the day and finding you all cuddled up next to him with my son."

If figurative statements were literal, half of Erica's face would've fell to the floor, it had cracked so badly. She stood staring at me, lips slightly parted, looking as though she was mind-testing words before she spoke them.

"Now what?" I said, sadly reveling in what had to have been nearly the saddest moment in my life. "Was your back hurting then? Did you call him over to give you a massage to fucking make it all better?"

"I'm sorry," she said, lowering her head. "It was a moment of weakness."

"What?" I yelled. "Like the moment of weakness when you let that motherfucker slide up in you and get you pregnant with David?"

Maybe it was the mention of his name, or the volume of my voice, but David opened his eyes and immediately started crying, wailing like a newborn.

148

"Now see what you did," Erica said, hurrying to the bed, scooping David up, rocking him in her arms, trying to calm him.

"What I did? What the fuck was that man doing in this house after all we've been through?" I was livid, going the hell off, fueled by anger and alcohol and good old-fashioned jealousy. "You told me you'd never see him again."

"I didn't know he was coming. He just showed up, wanting to see David and—"

"And you fucking allowed it?" I yelled, my speech slurring. "I told you what would happen if you ever let him in here again." And I was about to tell my wife just how deep in shit she was until I saw her going into the closet, David still on her hip, and pulling out a weekend bag. She set it on top of the dresser and started pulling clothes from one of the drawers: clothes she had obviously taken earlier from her drawers in our bedroom, like she had planned on living from this room for a few weeks.

"Hold it. What are you doing?" I said, fear in my voice.

"I obviously shouldn't be staying here anymore. I was right to be afraid of you. Me and David are going to leave for a while."

Those were the words I dreaded and feared hearing most. That was the reason I allowed all the Michael shit, the reason someone would've considered me a punk for looking the other way, swallowing actions most men would've probably killed their wives over. It was because she had the power to take David from me and I knew if I pushed her to hard, she would've done just that: what she's was about to do this very moment.

"Okay, okay, okay," I said, putting myself in front of her, palms up, trying to stop her. "I'm sorry. I shouldn't be yelling. There's just a lot going on right now. You don't have to go. Please don't go. Just stay here in this room. I'll go back to mine and I won't bother you again, okay?"

She looked at me as though she couldn't trust a word I had said, but nodded anyway and without saying a word, David still riding on her hip, Erica held open the door for me, showing me out.

In my room, I shed my clothes beside the bed after pulling my keys, wallet and cell phone out of my pockets, and setting them on the nightstand. I climbed in bed, lay butt ass naked on top of the comforter, not knowing just what happened, but hoping things would magically be better in the morning.

I closed my eyes, trying to rush sleep, when the room lit with the amber light from my cell phone screen. I turned, slapping a hand across the nightstand until I found it, held the phone high over my head to read a text message that said:

GOOD NIGHT, MURDERER

28

The next morning, I was at Serena's, sitting across from her at her kitchen table.

An hour earlier, alone in my house, staring out the living room window at my empty driveway, my phone to my ear, I said: "Are you gonna be home. I need to talk to you about something very important."

She released a worried sigh. "Is it about…"

"I'm afraid so. We need to talk. Like I said, it's very important."

I had brought Serena breakfast from McDonald's again, and she sat facing me at the table, the small bag torn open and used as a placemat for her breakfast burrito. She had not taken a bite; it sat there, the contents of a small packet of hot sauce emptied beside it.

"How's Janis?" I asked, hesitating to tell her the news about the text messages I've been getting.

"A little better. I think she's realizing that maybe she was wasting her time with Rasul, and that the world won't come to an end now that he's gone."

"Good."

"What do you have to talk to me about, Stan?"

I dug my cell phone out of my pocket, brought up the first threatening text message I received from whoever was sending them, then set the phone beside my wife's torn McDonald's bag.

"Start there. Read all of them." There were twenty-nine total—six more when I woke up this morning: more comments about how I would be abused behind bars, and how I'd be an old man when I was finally released, if I survived the brutal incarceration.

Serena took the phone, read through several of the messages, shock drawing her mouth open, widening her eyes. She looked up at me horrified. "Who...who is this?"

"I don't know," I mumbled, no longer rattled by the messages, just exhausted. "They just keep coming."

"Then this person knows?" Serena said, holding the phone to me, as if on the screen there was a photo of the person terrorizing me.

"Yeah. I guess."

"Do you know who it is? It's not Pope, is it?"

"I asked him and checked his phone to make sure. It's not him, Serena."

"Did you tell anyone?"

I didn't answer right away, just stared back at her.

"Well did you?"

"Erica," I admitted, sadly.

Serena slapped a hand on the table and rose from her seat, shaking her head. "Dammit Stan, we're all going to jail." She paced away from me.

I stood up. "She won't tell anyone. I know her."

Serena spun back to face me. "And you thought you knew her when she continued to sleep with that married man. You thought you knew her when she let him get her pregnant. And you think you know

152

her while she continues to play games with David. You don't know her, Stan." Serena took two steps closer, putting herself right in my face. She grabbed me by the shirt. "You don't know a motherfucking thing about that woman. Right now, she could be sitting in front of a detective spilling her guts, telling them where to go to pick the two of us up."

The scene flashed vividly before my eyes. Erica was gone this morning. Was it so far out of the realm of possibility, considering all that was going on between us, that she would do something like that? "No," I told Serena. "I'm telling you, you're wrong."

Pacing, arms fretfully folded, she said, "We have to get out of here. We just have to go."

I stood in front of her, blocking her next step. "What are you talking about?"

"We can pack our things: all of us: you, me and Janis. We can just go. We have money in the bank. We'll find jobs."

"Go where?"

"Mexico. Somewhere they won't come looking for us."

It was crazy talk, what I should've considered babel from someone who had lost her mind, but Serena was completely sane and sincerely serious.

"I'm telling you, Erica would never—"

"But what if you're wrong?" Serena said, pulling on my arms, pleading. "What would be so bad about the three of us leaving this place? It doesn't have to be another country. Another city, another state would be fine. It would be us again. Get you away from that woman, from that boy she's dangling like a carrot in front of you. We can do it."

She lay her palm against my cheek. "I loved you before. Who knows..." she smiled. "I still might. Tell me you can't love me again, that you don't still have some feelings for me." She stared at me: long lashes, smooth skin, full lips.

I wondered where we would've been if we hadn't allowed things in our past to tear us apart, wondered if our daughter would've ever gotten mixed up with a clown like Rasul if I had been her father full time. I touched Serena's face.

"There are some feelings I do still have for you," I admitted.

Gratitude turned up the corner of her mouth. She raised up on her toes, leaned toward me. I didn't know if it was me showing gratitude for her helping me through this horrible period, or if I truly had the desire to kiss her, but I leaned in and gently pressed my lips to hers.

Serena's eyes were closed when I pulled away from her. "I'll do something to fix this. As soon as I do, I'll let you know."

She silently stared at me, worry in her eyes, but there was also trust. She's known me for years, knew that when I said I would take care of a matter, I meant it, and she could rest assured it would happen.

Walking to my truck, I shook my head, looking back at the house, wondering what had just happened. I wasn't certain what motivated that, but for the first time in what felt like weeks, I felt myself smiling.

"Whatever," I said, shaking off the goofy grin, and the equally goofy feeling a teenaged boy might get when he falls for a girl he just met.

Before approaching my truck, I checked my cell phone, making sure it was on, because I hadn't gotten one of the troubling text messages in hours. I knew it was too much to hope for, but maybe they had just stopped.

I turned around, glanced back at the house, making sure Serena wasn't at the front door, looking back at me, then I decided I'd make another attempt at reaching Michael.

The phone ringing in my ear, I told myself this time when I got his voicemail, I'd leave a message. Things were getting so bad between Erica and I there was no longer time to play games. I needed to have a face to face with this man. That needed to happen now. I would leave those exact words on his machine. But to my surprise, the phone stopped ringing after the fourth ring. I heard a click, then a voice come on the line saying, "Hello, this is Michael."

29

I watched him through the glass doors as he walked toward me wearing a brown suit, white shirt and a purple speckled tie. He pushed his way inside the fast food, burger restaurant; it was where he said he wanted to meet: "The Varsity on North Avenue. You know where that is, right? I feel like a burger," he said, after we had been on the phone for only a minute. His tone was easy-going, as though talking to an old friend, not the man who was fathering his son.

I stood near the order counter: an all black staff, wearing white uniforms and matching white paper hats, loudly called out meal orders, grinning demonstrably, eagerly waiting on the next order. Michael stepped beside me, not looking at me, but at the lighted overhead menu.

"You hungry?" he said, rubbing his chin. "I'm hungry." He stepped up to the line without saying another word. I followed. When he was finished placing his order, he asked if I wanted something. I told the aging, short black man behind the register that I wasn't hungry. Michael took a step back from the counter and told me with a smile that the food won't pay for itself.

Outside, we stood in the shade of a parking structure behind the restaurant, vacant cars parked around us. Michael chewed the bite he took from the unwrapped burger he held in one hand, then pulled from the large strawberry milkshake he held in the other.

I stared hatefully at the side of his face as his jaw muscles flexed around the food.

"You were in my house the other day," I said. "Why?"

"Mmm, mmm," he said, holding up his shake, as if needing a moment. He swallowed the food he had in his mouth, slurped some of the shake, then: "Sorry. Didn't want to talk with my mouth full." He flashed an apologetic smile. "We have a problem, Stan. Is it okay if I call you Stan?"

"I don't give a fuck."

"Good. Like I was saying, we have a problem, Stan. As I'm sure Erica told you, my family is dead: my wife, my two kids—gone." He stared at me, paused a moment, as if that was the place he expected me to insert my heartfelt condolences. It didn't happen. He continued. "That fire took everyone I had, everyone I loved—killed my bloodline: but it kinda didn't. I still have a son," Michael said, keeping his eyes on me as he wrapped his lips around the straw and took another pull.

"No. David's my son. You signed your rights away."

Michael was into another huge bite of his sandwich, was chewing when he said, "True, true. I did sign them away, but now I want them back; I want my son back. That's why I was in your house. I'm getting to know David so when he's returned to me, things won't feel...how should I say—awkward."

I felt as though I would explode, not understanding how this man could appear so carefree and confident, like he was certain I'd just hand David back to him because he asked. I pointed a finger in his face. It trembled, I was so furious. "You're fucking out of your mind. If I catch you in my house again, if you call my wife, or attempt to see my son, I swear there will be no giving you a second warning. There will be no calling the police. I will just kill you. You understand me?"

He nodded, eyes on me as he drank from his shake. "I understand your passion," he said, tilting his cup, pointing at me with the tip of his straw, "But despite all that you just said, this is what you're going to do. You're going to go to a lawyer, draw up whatever paperwork is necessary to revert all of my fatherly rights back to me. You're going to sign those contracts, give them to me and then you're going to move out of Erica's house and you will give her a divorce. Do you understand?" He asked, peeking between the buns of his half eaten burger, pulling out a pickle slice and popping it into his mouth.

"You're clearly out of your mind. But if you come around my family again, don't say I didn't warn you of the consequences." I turned to walk away.

"Hold it, hold it, Stan!" Michael said, stepping over to a metal garbage can and dumping his burger and shake. "I have to do one thing," he said, wiping the crumbs from his hands, then reaching into his pocket and pulling out his cell phone. He tapped the screen several times. He was calling my wife, was going to have her order me to do the craziness he was insisting on, have her confess that it was Michael she wanted and not me. But instead of pressing the phone to his ear, he slid it back into his pocket then smiled at me.

"You're fucking crazy." I started walking off again: took a step then my phone vibrated in my pocket. I pulled it out as I continued away

159

from Michael, looking down at the message: another from the person who knew my secret:

GIVE DAVID BACK TO ME OR THE POLICE WILL KNOW YOU KILLED RASUL

I halted on the sidewalk beside the burger restaurant, my back to Michael, my stomach feeling queasy, my head starting to spin. Finally finding enough the courage to turn, I prayed what my mind was telling me wasn't true.

Michael was nodding, smiling. "That's right, Stan. It was killing me knowing there was no way you'd give me my son back after I foolishly gave him up. But when Erica told me you killed that boy, I realized with this information, you'd have choice but do what I say."

30

Hunched over the steering wheel, griping it with the intensity to crumble it in my fists, I raced home, blowing through yellow lights and hitting corners so fast I nearly flipped the Volvo over. I needed to get home, needed Erica to be there so that I could confront her about giving that man information that could put me away.

I slammed on the brakes in front of my house, the back end of the truck hiking up as I simultaneously yanked the key from the ignition and threw the driver's door open. Running up the walk, I saw that Erica's car was in the drive. She was there. What has been going on for so long would finally be brought to light.

Inside the house, I slammed the door with enough force to rattle the pictures hanging on the walls.

"Erica!" I yelled from the foot of the stairs, waiting a moment, expecting her to hear the rage in my voice: expecting to hear rustling about up there, then her footsteps overhead, hurrying toward the stairs. I expected her to apologize profusely, not knowing for exactly what, but knowing it had something to do with the lies she's been telling, and her elaborate plan to help Michael take my son.

But I stood, hearing nothing. "Erica!" I called again, louder, more forceful than the first time. I started up the stairs, hearing a drawer close in one of the rooms.

I trotted down the hallway to our bedroom, stopping in the doorway when I saw Erica in the room wearing only a bath towel, droplets of water rolling down her skin and clinging to the ends of her hair. I was momentarily thrown off by her beauty: it froze me only for a second, then I felt myself moving forward, sidestepping the bed, grabbing her by the shoulders, bulldozing her backward till her back hit the wall.

"You told him?" I yelled, furiously. "You told him that I murdered that boy? Why would you do that?"

"Stan!" She cried, trying to beat my hands off of her.

"You told him! Why?" I yelled, shaking her, the back of her head bumping against the wall behind her. "Do you know what he's trying to do to me?" I said, Michael's smug smirk appearing before my eyes, that overly confident tone of his voice ringing in my ears. "He's trying to blackmail me. He's trying to take David from me!" My wife's eyes were filled with terror. She stared at me: her husband, as though I was a stranger, when just the other day she was holding Michael: the real intruder, allowing him to hold our son. That had only happened because my wife encouraged him, made him think there was an opening for him. I felt my hands moving from her shoulders to her throat. They locked around it, and from outside of myself, I watched the scene from behind me: my arms outstretched, elbows locked, my hands wrapped around her neck, her wet hair whipping about her face with the violent turns of her head, the towel slipping, exposing one of her breasts as she screamed and coughed.

"You did this!" I yelled, not wanting to hurt her, but needing her to understand how much she hurt me. "You're letting him destroy this family," I said, tightening the lock I had on her neck.

She gasped and fought harder, then finally drove her left knee deep and hard into my grown. Debilitating pain stretched to every corner of my body. Blistering sparks of white exploded behind my closed eyes as my hands fell from her neck and I crumpled to the floor on my knees. I toppled onto my side, my arms folded into my middle, grabbing my aching stomach.

Tears spilling from eyes, I looked up at her; she stood fearlessly above me, tightening the towel over her breasts, catching her breath from what I had just put her through.

"He's...he's going to tell the police if..." I shut my eyes again, waiting for a brief stab of pain to calm. "If I don't give him David back...he's going to tell the police."

I stared at her to see if what I just said registered on her face. Her eyes rolled up; she looked as though she hadn't meant for things to go this way. She shook her head then sat on the mattress.

"Why...why did you tell him?" The pain from Erica's groin shot was slowly subsiding, enough for me to sit up, slide across the carpet and lean against a wall.

She was looking off in her thoughts, seeming as though trying to determine if what she had done was smart or stupid. She shook her head. "I don't know. If I had told you I had just murdered someone, you would've needed to tell someone: probably your ex-wife. It's the same thing"

"It's not the same. He was never your husband."

"He was the man I was seeing for ten years, and he's—"

She abruptly stopped herself.

"And he's the father of your child. That's what you were going to say, right?"

Her turning away from me, not replying, was just like her answering "yes". Didn't she know that? "So you're just not going to say anything?"

She looked sympathetically down at me. "I'm sorry this is happening. I am."

"He said he's going to tell the police if I don't do what he says. Did you hear me tell you that?"

"I heard you," Erica said, dropping her forehead in her palm.

"I'd go to jail if I don't do it," I said, feeling the possibility becoming more a reality the more I said it. "I can't go to jai, Erica. I'd lose—"

"Then maybe you should do what he says."

Silence. My words hung in my throat; I felt I couldn't breath. I sat up straighter against the wall. Shocked, I said, "What did you say?"

She looked at me a long moment before saying, "Which would you rather do: lose David or go to prison?"

"Wha...what?" I said, slowly and painfully getting to my feet. "Neither, Erica. Neither! When did those become my only options?" I said, stepping toward her. She leaned away, as though not wanting me near her. I kept my distance. "Why are you saying these things? David's my son. I love him."

"Do you? There was a time when you couldn't stand him, when I had to push him on you; you wanted nothing to do with him."

I wanted to say something to deny that, but I couldn't. "I love him now."

"You love the idea of him. He's a project for you. You messed up with Janis when she was younger and you look at David as a second chance: a do-over, your opportunity to raise him better than you were raised because you were abandoned by your father. But you've never loved him like a real father—like his real father loves him."

The statement had me needing to reach back a hand, find the dresser to brace myself against the feeling I might fall. "So you want this to happen? For me to be out of David's life?"

She averted her eyes. "You'll always resent him for not being yours. This is what'll take for that not to happen. So, yes," she said, setting her eyes back on me. "You need to be out of David's life."

"No," I said softly to myself, shaking my head. Then louder... "No! I'm not going to let this happen. I told you I'd kill for my family. I'd die before I'd let someone take him away from me."

Erica stood, holding her towel together, looking pathetically at me. "It's your choice, Stan. But make the wrong one, you might die in prison."

31

After Pope opened his front door, he knew immediately something was wrong with me. He was still wearing his work clothes; I had actually been sitting down street from his house, waiting for him to get home. I gave him five minutes after I saw him walk in to greet his wife and girls before hitting him with the horrible news I had found out.

"What happened?" he said.

"Come out here," I said. "We need to talk."

Pope looked back over his shoulder, yelled to his wife that he was stepping outside. He closed the door behind him and started down the stairs. On the street, outside his house, Pope turned to me, concern in his eyes. "What happened?"

"It was Erica," I said sadly.

"Erica's been sending the text messages?" Pope said, his voice rising an octave.

"No. She told Michael about the murder, and he's been—"

"Wait! How could she tell him when you said no one else knew?"

My head hung, I explained the confession I made in my sleep, my foolish belief that my wife would've kept the secret, and the fucked up situation I was in, because she hadn't.

Pope slapped his palms on his head, walked away from me, sighing. Walking back, he said, "So he's trying to get you to give up David? And Erica's not stopping him."

"I told you, she's the one that told him about what we…I mean, what I did. I never mentioned your name."

He appeared somewhat relieved. "I can't believe she'd allow this, after how well you treated David."

"Not always."

"That was then. And you had every right. She went out there, fucked around and you accepted David as your own, not only because that's the guy you are, but because she said you should: because she said David was *your* son! And now she does this." He turned his back on me again. "That's bullshit, Stan. Straight bullshit." He faced me. "She ask for a divorce?"

"There was no mention of that, but I figure it's coming. Pope, I can't lose my family this way."

Pope stared at me a long, sympathetic moment then said, "Well, don't do it."

"Don't do what?"

"Give David back."

"But—"

"But what, Stan?" Pope said, walking right up on me. "What does this Michael motherfucker know beside what you told Erica? He heard rumor of a murder, but does he know Rasul? Has he ever seen the boy?"

"No, but—"

"What proof does he or your wife have that any of what you said actually happened?"

"I confessed in my sleep and again the next morning."

"Her word against yours, my friend," Pope said.

"I don't know," I said, stopping myself from getting excited, feeling that Pope might've had a point.

"What do you mean, you don't know?" he said grabbing me by the arm. "You gonna let him win? Just let this bastard lay claim to your wife and child after cheating on his own family for a decade. No! You've done nothing wrong. As a matter of fact, you did everything right: loved your wife after she cheated on you: raised her child as your own: been nothing but the devoted husband and father, only to bend to that motherfucker's demands? No way! You're not signing away your rights."

"Hell no, I won't!" I said.

"You're gonna tell that motherfukcer Michael what to do with those papers he wants you to sign, right?" Pope said, holding out a hand to me.

I slapped my hand in his. "You goddamn right."

We held firmly to the others hand, staring into the others eyes, realizing the risk we were taking, but having faith that what we told ourselves was correct: there was no evidence, so there was no murder: at least not one that could be proven. At least that's what we had hoped.

32

I had to admit, I felt better leaving Pope's place.

I had received his customary hug, then him holding me at arm's length, he smiled, clapped me on the shoulder: "We gonna get through this, right."

I smiled to. "I think we are," I nodded. "Yeah, I think so."

Driving away, I told myself I didn't know how things would work out with Erica. She had every right to divorce me if she felt she had to, but she would not force me out of my son's life.

My cell phone rang—Serena on the phone, her voice calm: "I think you need to come over here."

"Everything all right?" I asked, immediately unsettled. "Is Janis okay?"

"Just come, Stan."

I drove there as fast as I could, and closed the front door after Serena let me. She had said nothing to me, so I stood there, not knowing what to expect.

"C'mon in, have a seat," she finally said, stepping out of the living room, leaving me there. A moment later, she came back in with a bottle of white liquor and two short glasses. She set the glasses on the coffee table, poured them each a quarter full and held one out to me. The somber mood in the room told me these weren't celebratory drinks.

"What is this?" I said, holding the glass.

"Drink it and I'll tell you."

We turned up our glasses together, drained them and set them on the table.

"Someone came to visit me today," Serena said, setting her glass down.

"What? Who?" I said, sliding to the edge of my seat.

She shook her head, picked up the bottle and poured another shot in our glasses. "Just listen and let me tell you everything."

I took my glass, held it in my palm as she told me how a man rang the doorbell earlier. She said he was neatly shaven, wore a suit and tie and asked if he could come in. She told him no. He told her he believed it was in her best interest that she did. She stepped aside and he took two steps into the living room then stopped, staring at the walls. Serena demanded to know what he wanted.

He told her who he was, then pointed to the bare TV bracket mounted to the wall over the fireplace and to the vacant spaces on the walls where there were once framed pictures. Michael then smiled slyly, as if knowing something that should've been kept secret.

"This is where it happened, isn't it?" he said.

Serena asked what he was talking about.

"The fight: your ex-husband wrestling with the boy, the two of them bouncing off the walls making the pictures fall," Michael said, pointing to the walls where the absent pictures once were. "They end up over here by the fireplace. I don't know, maybe one of them reaches up, grabs the TV for leverage, pulls it down by accident. Or maybe, as a threatening show of force, the boy snatches it down before the fight even starts. Your husband and the boy tussle some more, fight for the gun, land here," Michael said, pointing down to the brick landing in front of the fireplace. Your ex-husband gets the upper hand, knocks the poor boy's head against this stone floor here and, accidently or intentionally, kills him." Michael bends a little at the waist, as if to closer examine the carpet beside the landing. "Yeah, there's some discoloration there." He looked over at Serena, smiling. "Yeah, I think that's what could've happened, but I could be wrong. I watch a lot of CSI, solve all the puzzles way before the end of the show. But like I said, I could be wrong."

Serena told me she watched him walk across the room, sit where I was now sitting, then he very politely asked her to have a seat. He told her that he had spoken to me and asked that I do him a very simple favor, but he believed that I wouldn't give him what he wanted. He believed that I thought there wasn't enough proof to land me in prison. "He thinks it's just my word against his. But I've done a little research on Mr. Rasul Washington," Michael told Serena. "He has a grandmother that lives in the West End. I caught her outside doing some gardening yesterday. Lied to her, told her I was his employer, said I hadn't seen him in a week. She told me she hadn't seen him in a while either. That it wasn't like him to just up and disappear without calling her at least once a day. I asked her for his phone number, then I had a good friend at Verion give me Rasul's phone records," Serena told me Michael said, as he pulled the papers out of his inside jacket pocket, shaking his head. "Kids today: ending relationship via text. How inconsiderate."

Serena said he tossed the records on the table in front of her then said, "Considering how crazy in love that boy was supposed to be with your daughter, and the fact she's having his baby, I can't see him just dumping her like that, especially the day after he had been killed."

He told Serena that he knew the phone records proved nothing, that his word meant nothing, and that Rasul's grandmother knew nothing. But, "If I cause enough commotion, like, let's say telling your daughter that her father might've killed Rasul and telling the same thing to the boy's grandmother, maybe just maybe, some superhero-detective-of-the-month might want to investigate." Michael dug out his cell phone, tapped and swiped at the screen a few times, then held it out to Serena. "Oh yeah, and there's this."

Serena looked up at me now and said, "It was a picture of the shirt and pants you were wearing the night Rasul died. There were close up shots of blood on them. How did he get your clothes, Stan?"

"What?" I said, my mind spinning. "I threw them away that night, and—Erica! She could've..." An image of her stepping out the back door, fishing out the clothes after I had climbed back up the stairs, played across my mind. "It had to have been her."

Serena lowered her head, set the glass of alcohol down, as though realizing no amount of liquor could fix this situation. "He said he'd give the clothes to the police."

"I'm sorry, Serena. I'm so sorry."

She looked up at me as though exhausted by this situation, as though exhausted by me. "What is this favor he asked you to do to make this all go away?"

"That I sign my rights to David back over to him. If I don't, he'll go to the police, which means I might go to jail."

Serena turned away from me, looked around the room for nothing in particular, or just for an excuse not to look at me. She lifted her glass, drained it, set it back down then said, "Then I guess you need to do as he says."

33

I stared at the closed elevator doors as the machine carried me up to the 23rd floor where my father's law offices were located. It was past closing time, but I knew he often worked late: I *needed* him to be working late.

I stared anxiously up at the numbers above the elevator doors: a higher number lighting with each floor I ascended. My fists shook at my side as I tried to squelch the anger and feeling of utter helplessness growing within me. I thought it sad that both my ex-wife and my current wife gave me the same advice in regard to how I should handle the situation with Michael: give the man what he wanted.

The doors slid open; I squeezed between them before they fully parted. I ran down the hallway, stopped at the outer door to my father's offices when I saw his secretary standing on high heels about to lock the door with a key.

"Is he in there?"

She knew me, knew that I was her boss's son. "Yes, but we're closing and—"

"Doesn't matter," I said, as respectfully as possible, pushing around her and grabbing the doorknob. "I need to see him. I'll let him know you tried to stop me, okay."

She nodded her head. "Fine."

I knocked lightly on my father's door. "Dad, it's me," I said, opening it.

From behind his desk, he looked up at me surprised, but seemingly pleased to see me. I closed the door behind me, and for some reason, locked it. Turning back to him, he was up out of his chair, making his way around his desk, concern on his face.

"Everything all right, Stan?"

"I need a contract drawn up."

I had made up my mind on the way over here—hell, on the steps outside of Serena's house, before leaving her. "You are going to do what he said, right?" Serena asked, appearing saddened and beaten up as I had felt, as though Michael had physically assaulted the both of us, whooped our asses with his threats. She was concerned about me going to jail, about her being dragged off too, and worried all of that would leave our daughter without the parents she so desperately needed now.

"Yeah, Serena," I nodded sadly, conceding. "I'm gonna do what he says."

In my father's office, Dad asked, "You need a contract? For what?"

In the two years since I've been back in my father's life, he's grown to love David nearly as much as I have. He'd take David on Sundays to the zoo, or for ice cream or to see the baseball stadium to see the Braves play, always calling in the evening, asking if he could keep him overnight and bring him back Monday morning. When I told him no, that David had to be up for daycare the next day, my father would begrudgingly bring him home: David asleep, his head resting on my father's shoulder. And when Dad would gently pass him over to me, he'd thank me for pushing my way back into his life, for having such a wonderful son, and doing the right thing: not running off when I found out the child wasn't mine, but manning up and being the boy's father.

"I'm signing my parental rights back over to the biological father," I told Dad.

"What?" Dad gasped. "Why in the world would you ever do that?"

"I have my reasons. Are you able—"

"Why, Stan?" He asked, stepping closer to me. I turned a shoulder on him, not wanting to engage him in this argument. "Because I just have to," I mumbled.

"Stan, you need to tell me why you're doing this."

I felt his hand on my shoulder. "No, I don't." I shrugged him off, caught sight of the liquor bottles stacked on the tray across the room, knew that's what I needed and started toward them.

"Stan—"

"No, Dad."

Before I made it to the bottles lined up on the cart, I felt my father's hands on me again, spinning me around to face him. I didn't resist him. I felt like a child in his grip, felt like I had been bested by the bully at school, wanted to cry on my dad's chest, beg him to make things better. But I knew that was impossible. I tried to pull away from him once more.

He tightened his grip, shook me. "This is my office! You want my help, you tell me why you're trying to make such a goddamn stupid decision as to give up my grandson!"

"Because I killed someone, okay!" I yelled, fed up. "I killed someone, got rid of the body, and Erica told David's father, and now he's threatening to blackmail me." My chest heaving, I felt my father's fists loosen from around my shirt. Releasing me, he took a step back, but not as though repulsed, but sympathetically, as if knowing I had to have been forced into doing such a terrible thing.

I turned to the bar, uncorked the first bottle I put a hand on, sloppily spilled some of it's contents into a glass, brought it to my mouth and gulped it down. I refilled the glass before having the nerve to face my father again. When I did, he looked at me deflated, as though he had failed me, as though by leaving me, he had made me a murderer.

"The boy your daughter was seeing?" He asked. "The one you told me about?"

Glass to my lips, I nodded.

"Was he that bad of a person?" Dad asked.

I set the empty glass down behind me. "He threatened Serena with a knife and pulled a gun on me. It was only a matter of time before he would've hurt Janis. I didn't wanna kill him, Dad," I said, the enormous weight of what I did returning, as though Pope and I had just dug the boy's ditch last night, as though I could still feel the sticky slickness of Rasul's blood on my fingertips.

"Okay, son," he said. "It's okay. But is it taken care of, right? And no one will find out if you do what this Michael—"

"I don't want to lose my boy," I said, breaking down, realizing what I was about to do, what I was being forced to do.

"I know you don't. I know," Dad said, holding me, as I clutched onto his back and sobbed on his shoulder, wishing I could make all of this disappear, that I could wake from a dream and return to the life that made sense.

"I know you don't," Dad said. "But it seems you have no choice."

34

Inside my truck, I stared up at my house while waiting for my call to be answered.

"Hello," the voice on the other end I had grown to hate, answered.

"You went by my ex-wife's house, made reference to my daughter," I said, still fuming at the thought of that. "This is between us. You had no right going over there."

"You're right, Stan," Michael said. "I just needed to let you know how serious this all is, and that there will be swift and definite consequences if you don't do what I'm asking. You got the contracts drawn up?"

My eyes shut, the phone pressed to my ear, I said, "They'll be done sometime tomorrow."

"You'll call me when you've got them," he said. "I want to get this thing over with so I can have my son back, you understand?"

I shut my eyes again, tightened my grip around the phone and bit down on my lip as if against a searing physical pain. I forced myself not to speak, just brought the phone down from my ear and disconnected the call.

When I walked in the house, it was quiet, save for the sound of movement in the kitchen. I started to call out to Erica like I usually did, but things weren't the same: they were as far away from the same as they could ever be.

I stopped in the kitchen doorway, cleared my voice to get her attention, for she hadn't noticed me there behind her. Obviously she hadn't been listening out for me, hadn't been looking forward to me coming home. I was sure there were other things on her mind; I hated to think that the man extorting me was one of them.

Erica looked up from the salad she was putting together in a bowl: enough for only one. "Hey," she said, then her attention returning immediately to the tomatoes she was cutting.

"I did what you asked," I said from the doorway, almost afraid to step into the room with her for fear of her asking me to step out. "The contracts are being drawn up for me to sign."

"If that's what you decided to do," Erica said, looking up again, about to slice into a cucumber.

"No. It's not what I decided to do. You gave him information that's allowing him to force me to do this."

She held my sad stare for a long moment, then without a word, lowered her head and went back to her chopping.

I stood thinking of what else to say, but there was no wining this argument with her: nothing I could do to change this situation. I was powerless. We both knew it. "Is David upstairs?" I asked.

"Yes."

"In *his* room?"

"Yes," she answered for the second time, neither of which she looked me in the eyes.

My tone measured and hopeful, I said, "Since he'll only be my son for one more night, would you mind if I go up and spend some time with him?"

She quickly grabbed the towel from the counter, as if to wipe her hands clean and accompany me.

"Alone. Please?" I said.

"Fine, Stan," she nodded. "Sure. Just try not to wake him up, please."

"I won't. And thank you." I was about to walk away, but there was something I needed to address first. "What happened with us, Erica?"

She had just sat down with her meal, fork and napkin. She sighed as though it had been an incredibly long day and she didn't want to deal with such trifles at mealtime.·

"We had this conversation already. There's nothing more to—"

"We've been married for years. We have a son together...at least for the moment. All of that is about to end, and one short conversation is all you think I deserve. Erica, I gave my heart to you. I've never cheated on you, even though I had every fucking right to after what you did, and after all that, I raised yours and that man's son like he was my own, because you said you wanted me to, because you said it was okay." I took two determined steps into the kitchen. "The very fucking least you could do is tell me what happened."

"Fine," Erica said, bawling up her napkin, dropping it in the bowl on top of her salad then shoving the dish aside. "What was the question again?"

I obviously still loved my wife, but that moment, I wanted to charge her, jump over that table and shake the shit out of her. Instead I asked: "What happened to us?"

"I took you because I couldn't have him," Erica said, sounding unapologetic.

How foolish had I been those three years ago when she told me she was having that man's baby not to have just run then, not to have seen this as a possible future. Now that it's happening, it seems foolish to think that things might've gone any other way.

"So you still love him?"

"I gave you the explanation you asked for. There's nothing else I have to say." She glanced over at her food, as though it was more important than I ever could've been.

"But he didn't choose you. I did. And like I was for you, you'll be the consolation prize for him. He would still be with his wife if she were alive, you know that don't you?"

"Doesn't matter," Erica said, dragging her bowl back in front of her, picking the napkin from off of it. "That's not my concern, because she's no longer alive."

Upstairs, I stood outside David's room, my hand sweaty around the doorknob; I was terrified of entering, knowing how ridiculous it would've been to go in there just to further my torture. The man had already won; he had taken the son I considered mine away from me, as he had taken my wife before I had even met her. Go inside, fall to my knees at David's bedside, morn him like he had died? It made no sense, I thought, turning away from the door. I quickly whirled back around, filled with rage, anger and pent up frustration, swinging my arm, wanting to burry it, elbow deep into the door. I stopped myself, my knuckles less than an inch from the door's surface, crying out in silent agony. I walked away, down the hallway, trying to find an answer that would allow me to keep my family. Halting, I threw a gaze back at my son's room, truly accepting the fact there was nothing I could do. Don't make a bigger deal of this than what it is, I told myself, walked back then quietly pushed into my son's room to say goodbye.

35

I woke with a start, not knowing where I was. Looking around, I saw that I was still in my son's bed; I must've fallen asleep with him last night. I rolled over, my back aching from the hours spent curled up on the twin mattress, and realized he was no longer there with me. I quickly climbed out of bed, hurrying to the door, throwing it open, rushing down the hallway, down the steps, fearing that Erica had taken him and disappeared for good.

I stopped abruptly at the kitchen door, seeing him in his high chair, Erica gazing out the window, sipping from a coffee mug. She rotated, looked at me as though I was pathetic.

"Hi, Dawdy," David said.

"Hey Lil' Man," I said, going to him, caressing the back of his head, then kissing him on this face, wondering how long it would take for me to be forever lost from his memory. I said to Erica, spitefully: "You could've woken me when you took him."

"You were sleeping," she said, dismissively.

"So the fuck what!" I snapped. "I'm sorry, I'm sorry," I said to Erica, seeing David jump. I kissed his head again, apologized to him several more times.

Erica turned to fully face me, leaned against the sink, looking at me as though wishing she could speed time so all of this could be over with.

"So how does it happen?" I asked, walking up to her. "When I leave to pick up the papers, you start packing? Do you wait to leave here until after you hear from Michael that they're signed, or will you be waiting for him with my son at his hotel?"

"We're not having this conversation again," Erica said, brushing past me, heading for the door to the living room.

"We haven't talked about this before. You are divorcing me, right?" I said, quickly, before she exited the kitchen entirely.

She stopped, her back to me.

"After the two of you get David," I said. "You're going to file for divorce. That's the plan, right?"

"You know what? I'm done with this." She looked flustered and fed up. She walked quickly back into the kitchen, set her cup down on the nearest counter and made for David. She edged me out of the way with a hip, grabbed him from under the arms and hoisted him onto her chest.

"What are you doing?" I asked, feeling there was a shift for the worst that had just occurred.

"I'm taking him to day care."

"No! Let me." My hours were numbered with him; after today I might not have another opportunity to see him, let alone spend time with him by myself.

"No," Erica said.

"Why not?"

"I don't need to give you an explanation."

"He's still my son. Legally, I'm still his father. Please Erica," I begged, reaching out to her, trying to appeal to the woman that once loved me. "Do you hate me that much now that you won't even allow this?"

She sighed heavily, her shoulder's slumping, as though dealing with me was the worst drudgery she's ever experienced. "I don't hate you, Stan," she said. "It's just that this is over and there is absolutely nothing you can do about it."

36

After Erica left with David, I spent the morning sitting for hours in different rooms of the house—our bedroom, David's room, the living room, the kitchen—staring at the walls, out the windows, into my memory, laughing sadly every now and then at the wonderful times first Erica and I had, then times the three of us shared as a family: moments I'd never forget.

Every time I heard a car outside, I rushed down the hallway, or down the stairs—depending on which room I sat—and pulled back the curtain, thinking it might've been Erica, that she had rethought things, had a change of heart about divorcing me, or at least chose to bring David back so that I could see him one last time. Each time that happened, I walked away from the window disappointed, my head hung.

Later that afternoon, my father had called, told me the contracts were ready.

After I got there and after he set them out in front of me on his desk, I stood over them, a pen shaking in my hand, my father looking over my shoulder.

"Are you sure this is really what you want to do?"

I looked up at him. "You mean give my son away? This is not meant as an attack on you. I'm just asking a question," I said. "But was it easy for you to just give me up?"

"I was young, and nothing or no one was more important than me. I didn't think twice about leaving you. But looking back, thinking about all the years I've lost with you, years that I can never get back: I regret that decision every minute of the day." He reached down, grabbed my hand then eased the pen out of it. "Don't do this yet, son. There's still time. Think through all your options, and make sure there is absolutely nothing you can do to avoid losing your boy, regardless how out-of-this-world, illogical or dangerous it might seem."

I hugged my father goodbye, drove to a run-down, questionable part of town, slumped in the seat of my truck, feeling sorry for myself. I thought about never seeing my son again. I thought about my daughter and the potential she might've gotten harmed by Rasul, and finally I thought about Rasul himself: his face pointed skyward as he lay dead on the grass, eyes open, the ax at the apex of Pope's swing, just before it started downward. I thought about everything that was done to protect my family against the outrageous acts of a man who had no right to them, but the audacity to commit those acts.

I pulled out my phone, feeling as though I had no choice, as though there was a gun to my head. I dialed the number, pressed it to my ear, listened as it rang. My eyes closed, I prayed he wouldn't answer. Upon hearing his voice, I felt my depression deepen. "I have the contracts," I said.

"You sign them?"

I opened my eyes. The sun was setting, the sky turning a deep shade of violet. "I'll do that with you there...so you can see."

"That's a good idea," Michael said. "Bring them to—"

"No," I interrupted, wielding what little power I had left. "You want the papers, you go where I tell you."

It was after nine when I rolled slowly over the gravel in the vacant parking lot, behind a towering abandoned building: black squares in the crumbling brick façade, jagged shards of broken windows in the panes

I pulled the Volvo to a stop fifteen feet away from the black Infiniti. The engine was off; I could see the gold glow of the car's dash lights, hear the faint sound of a John Legend song seeping from the open windows. I hated John Legend.

I shut off my truck, picked up the manila envelope Dad slid the unsigned contracts in, and pushed my way out. Tiny rocks crunching under my shoes, this was where I told Michael to meet me when we spoke on the phone earlier. It was an industrial warehouse park. There wasn't a soul in sight.

"That's in the middle of nowhere," he said after I gave him the address.

I said nothing, just held the phone to my ear, letting him know the meeting place was non-negotiable.

The downtown skyline was in the distant background: tiny lights taking the shape of rectangular buildings. Squat, one-story warehouses surrounded the lot, encircling us within a radius of a fifty-foot circle.

I walked up and around the front of his car toward the passenger door.

"Been here twenty minutes," he said, as I passed. "Thought you were trying not to show."

"I'm here," I said, grabbing the handle. He pressed a button on his door, unlocking it. I lowered myself into the car, pulling the door closed.

"Those them?" Michael said, his eyes on the envelope I held.

I waited till the dome light dimmed and went black inside the car before saying, "Yeah, but I don't have a pen."

He smiled as if this was a motherfucking joke. He flipped open the top of his armrest and produced something to write with. "The least I can do," he said, holding out a hand. "The contract, please."

"Where are the clothes?"

Michael nodded toward the back seat.

I shifted to get a look. They were there, in the same big, plastic Zip-lock bag they were in in the cell phone pictures. I handed him the envelope and Michael slid the papers out, turning on an overhead map light. Checking them out, his eyes slowly moving left to right, he said, "Anyone else would have their attorney look these over first." He paused, as though paying closer attention to a specific clause, then resumed his browsing. "But knowing what I have on you, I assume I don't have to worry about any game playing, do I?" His eyes were up off the page and on me.

"I'm not here to play games."

Another shit-eating smile from him, then his eyes dropped back to the pages. I stared at him, loathing everything about him: the smell of him, the color of his skin, the fabric of his shirt, the way he sat in his seat: his knees bent just under the dash, the almost silent in-and-out of his breathing as he continued to read the contract that would destroy the life I've known for the last four years.

"Where were you that night?" I asked.

"What are you talking about?" Michael said, not looking up.

"The night your family burned in your house. Erica said you didn't get home till after one in the morning. Where were you?"

"That's none of your—"

"You don't have to say. I already know: probably out fucking someone else's wife."

He bristled at my comment, but said nothing.

"Why didn't you go in to save them?" I asked.

"The house was totally on fire," he said, as though resenting his need to explain to me his inaction.

"They could've still been alive. If you would've just gone in...they might still be alive right now. But you didn't, because you're not a good man."

"You don't know what the fuck you're talking about," Michael said, tossing the pages up on the dash, twisting in his seat to face me.

"I don't? You cheated on your wife for ten years. You had a baby outside of your marriage with *my* wife. You were a fucking stain on my life before I ever knew who you were," I said, raising my voice as I felt myself starting to lose control of my anger. "I thought I had found my soul mate, but my marriage was destined to fail because of you," I said, turning away.

"Your marriage failed because you let it," Michael said.

I barely heard him. I was off in my head, staring out the windshield into the dark vacant corners around us, counting all the ways he had destroyed what I loved most.

"You signed those papers and said David would be my son." My voice was low, just loud enough for him to hear. "But here you are, wanting him back. You were to stay away from my wife, but you've been seeing her; you were in my fucking house." I cut a narrow-eyed stare at him, holding it for not even a second, then looked back out the windshield. "No. You are not a good man. You have trespassed all over my life, disrupted my family, disrespected me as a man as though there would be no consequences: as though I'd just fucking go along."

Michael glanced at the papers on the dash, then back at me, carefree, discounting the extreme seriousness of all I had just said. "Stan, it's too let to grow balls now. You're signing this contract," he said, reaching for them. One fell to the floor under the dash. "Or else I'll go to the police and…

I watched him grope blindly for the fallen page, thinking that I had every right to do what was about to be done.

Let me back up a moment.

Earlier on the phone, I had told Michael I needed an hour before we meet, knowing I would make a trip home before seeing him. Once there, in the room I would soon no longer share with Erica, I sat on the bed, an open shoebox beside me, the contents in my hand.

The night Rasul died, after helping Pope carry the boy's body out to the truck, I walked back into the living room and saw something peeking out from under the crumpled area rug. I looked toward the hallway, saw that Serena was still in the kitchen. I quickly bent down, picked up the item and pushed it into my pocket.

When its whereabouts came up, I lied and told Serena that Pope and I had thrown it off a bridge. When Pope asked, I had told him I buried it in field miles away from the house; that he needn't ever worry about it appearing again.

But sitting there in my room before my meeting with Michael, staring down at Rasul's gun, I told myself I must've believed the night of the boy's death, that I would've needed the weapon some day.

This was that day.

In the car, as Michael bent down to retrieve the fallen page of the contract from under the dash, I pulled the gun from my pocket.

Getting his hands on the page, he looked up at me, then at the dark hole in the gun's barrel, staring him in the face. He recoiled, slamming his back into the driver's side door.

"Wha...what the fuck!" His eyebrows pushed all the way up, his palms raised, fingertips trembling, he said, "What the hell are you doing?"

"You're blackmailing me for doing what?"

"What?" His question was a high-pitch squeal.

"What did I do that's allowing you to blackmail me?" I said, raising my voice.

"You killed that boy...Rasul."

"That's right. Do you know why?"

"I don't give a fuck, Stan!" Michael cried.

"He tried to take my daughter from me," I said, the gun still on Michael. "I killed a man because he fucked with my family, yet here you are, attempting the same thing, as though I wouldn't defend David and

Erica the same way." I gave him a moment to let what I said sink in. "I am a man that has just committed murder, and yet, you play fucking games with me, as though you couldn't wind up dead yourself. How could you have never thought about that, Michael?" I said, raising the gun, holding it closer to his forehead.

"God no!" He whimpered. "I'll stop. You can have Erica! Keep David! We...we can tear up the contract right now!"

"You..." I paused surprised that it had been that easy. "You mean that?"

"Hell yeah, I mean it! I don't wanna die. Keep your family. I'll be fine. I'm moving to D.C. Erica told you, right? I'm getting the fuck out of here!" he cried nervously. "You'll never see me again."

Feeling the thinnest of smiles coming to my lips, one I forced myself to suppress, I could not believe that it was all over. I lowered the gun a little, feeling an enormous sense of relief. It was over! I would go home, tell Erica that Michael decided he didn't want the responsibility of her and David after all, that he decided to move to D.C. and on with the rest of his life by himself. She might not believe that, but I would convince her. And yes, there would be a rough period for us: there would be a lot of hard work and forgiving to do, but I believed we'd be able to work things out and keep our family together.

"So, yes?" Michael asked, his voice still quavering, his palms still up, his eyes still round and staring at the gun. "I'll fucking leave them alone. You'll never see me again."

Believing those were the best words I'd heard in my life, I felt everything was changing for the better, and I started to lower my gun when Michael finished by saying: "I promise."

That moment something snapped in me and I was back in my living room, three years ago when he said those exact words. "I promise," he said about never seeing Erica again. "I promise," he said about never trying to see David. And, "I promise," he said about never attempting to take my son from me. Those were his words, but he had lied then. A gun to his face, why should I believe that he wasn't lying now? That if I were to let him walk away, that after a short period of time, after he regrouped, he won't go at me again: tell the police I had threatened to kill him on top of having already killed someone else. That he won't keep after me until he takes what he wants, what's most dear to me. Yes, despite the promise he just made, I sensed Michael would not this go, because he wasn't a good man, and he hadn't kept a single one of the promises he had made in the past.

The gun trembled in my hands as I raised it, the sight on the barrel bisecting the space between his eyes. Goddammit, I thought, applying the slightest pressure on the trigger. Why couldn't he have left things alone when he had the chance?

"Okay. We have a deal, right. I'm gonna grab these papers off the dash and tear them up," he said. "Okay?"

"Yeah, okay," I said, asking for forgiveness from whoever could grant it.

"Good," he said as he went for the pages, the fear already sounding completely absent from his voice. He took the papers from the dash, saying, "I'm glad you came to your senses, Stan, because—"

Before he could finish, me having turned off the reasoning and compassionate part of my brain, I pulled the trigger, illuminating the corner of the desolate neighborhood where the black Infiniti sat. The cabin of the car lit up, a muffled pop was heard and blood, brain and tiny fragments of Michael's skull sprayed the window behind him.

37

I stood outside the car as a slowly approaching vehicle basked me in white headlamp light.

After I had pulled the trigger killing Michael, I sat listening for noises outside the car: silence. Surprisingly, my hands stopped shaking; they were relaxed around the gun. I lay the weapon against my thigh—it was warm—and stared at Michael. A streetlamp on a wooden pole thirty feet above provided enough light for me to see him: shoulders bunched up around his ears, his back pressed awkwardly against the car door, his tongue sticking, cartoon-like, out the corner of his mouth. The tiny bullet hole in his forehead leaked a line of blood that spilled thin and straight down the center of his face and clung in a bulb at the tip of his nose.

I had to get rid of the body. I pulled out my cell phone, started to dial Pope, but stopped—the light of the cell screen on my face—I realized he accepted me killing Rasul because the man was threatening my daughter, and it was in the act of self-defense. Michael's death was premeditated; I had called the man out to this exact spot so no one would hear the gunshot. Yes, Pope was my best friend. Our friendship was real, but his moral compass was much stronger than to go along with me killing someone to get them out the way. I couldn't risk him "doing the right thing". I cleared his name from the screen and swiped another.

Now, the approaching car stopped in front of me. The headlamps went dark and the door opened. When Serena walked up to me, she read the look on my face, the expression on hers saddened and she threw her arms around me.

"Dammit Stan," I heard her say, her warm breath against my ear. "Did you *have* to do it?"

"I don't know. Yes."

While I waited for her to come, I hoisted Michael's body from the driver's seat to the passenger side. It would be his car I'd use to transport the body, while Serena followed behind. Taking her hand, I walked her around to the passenger side of Michael's car. She told me she came as fast as she could, and that that the shovels and the ax I asked her to bring from the garage were in the trunk.

Still holding her hand, I said, "I'm sorry I had to call you. I didn't know if Pope would—"

"Shhh!" she said. "You should've called me first anyway. You should always call me first. You got that?"

"Yeah, I do now," I said, appreciatively. "You ready for this?" I said, reaching for the passenger door handle.

"No more than I'll ever be," she said.

Michael's phone rang at half hour intervals for two hours while we disposed of his body. The first time it rang, Serena took the phone out of his pocket, looked at the screen and said: "It's your wife...the conniving bitch. What do you want to do?" She held the phone up. I stared at the screen lit up with my wife's name. I wanted to answer it, tell Erica exactly what I had done, what she forced me to do; I wanted to take pics, kneel down there with Michael and take a fucking selfie while turning up the corners of his lips in a smile with my fingers. "Nothing. Let it ring," I said, getting a firm grip on the ax. "We need to concentrate on getting him buried."

It took us more than three hours to get rid of Michael the same way Pope and I had taken care of Rasul, in nearly the exact same location; I knew of nowhere else or no other way to dump a body. Before we left the burial site, I asked Serena if she had brought the gasoline I had asked for. She went into the trunk, brought out the can, passing it to me. "Be careful," was all she said.

I opened all the doors, doused the seats, the carpet inside. I poured gasoline over the roof, the hood and the trunk of Michael's car then set the thing on fire.

I pulled up in my car behind Serena, the two of us parking in front of her house. It was close to 11 o'clock. We cut off the engines, climbed out of the cars and met between them. She looked sympathetically at me, reaching out to take one of my hands. "I'm sorry this is happening. But you did what had to be done. He gave you no—"

"Nothing needs to be said. I'm fine with it," I said, squeezing her hand softly in appreciation of her being there for me.

"Come in. You can have some tea, or something stronger. I'm sure Janis is still up. She'd love to see you."

It was something I could've done: walk in the house in which I used to live, sit and talk to my family: my first family, and just never leave. Erica wouldn't have missed me. She probably wasn't even home, but wherever Michael was supposed to have returned to.

"I can't. I need to go home, deal with this thing with Erica. Try to save my marriage," I said, seeing how those last words saddened Serena.

She pulled her hand away from mine and looked away. "What I just helped you do, it's not to win any kind of competition. It's because you were once my husband, and still my friend. It's because you are the father of our daughter, and I will always care what happens to you."

"Serena, you don't have to—" I said, reaching for her hand again. Again, she pulled away.

"No, Stan, we having something."

"We do?" I questioned.

"Or we could, if you let us. But I won't continue hoping and wishing one day you'll see that I care more for you than that woman ever will. What we *could* have, I want. I want you back. I want Janis to have her father back. I want us to be a family again. I'm giving you the opportunity to make that happen. But walk away from me now," Serena said, brushing the tips of her fingers under an eye, "There won't be another chance, because I won't ever want to see you again."

"You aren't serious, Serena."

"I'm as serious as that dead body I just helped you put in the fucking ground," she said, staring me in the eyes, waiting for me to make my decision.

Shaking my head, I said, "I'm sorry, Serena. I have to go home to—

"

Before I could finish, she wrapped her arms around my neck, pressing her body to mine. "Goodbye Stan. I hope it all works out for you. I really do." She released me, walked to the house, opened the door and stepped inside, leaving me feeling as though I was abandoning her, abandoning my first family, and making the biggest mistake of my life.

I turned, about to pull open my car door, but stopped when I heard my daughter call me from the front door. She bounded down the stairs, stopping in front of me. "Where are you and Mom coming from?"

There was no way I could come close to telling her. "Nowhere," I said, lacking the energy to come up with anything better.

"Fine, you don't want to tell me. But where are you going?"

"Home," I said it as though there was reason to be ashamed. "I have to go home."

"I figured. I know you have to go home. Mom realizes that too, but for some reason she still has a thing for you," Janis said, hunching her shoulders, smiling just a little.

"For some reason, huh."

"She misses you."

"Do you miss me?"

Janis smiled wider. "Yeah, I guess I do." She hugged me. "And I'm not mad at you."

"For what?" I asked, easing away from her.

"Rasul didn't just up and leave because you were a pain in his ass. Something else happened that made him stop coming around, right?"

"I don't know, Janis. Maybe."

"It doesn't matter now. There was stuff he was involved in that you didn't know about. Bad stuff. He wasn't the best boy for me, and it took whatever you did to make him leave. I guess things are better when you're here."

"They are?" I asked, surprised, never having heard that from Serena or Janis.

"Yeah Dad, they are. So don't worry about what Mom just told you. If you wanna come back, Dad. Just come back.

38

When I went to slip my key into the front door our house, Erica was there. She yanked it open, worry on her face.

"Expecting someone else?" I said, walking past her toward the stairs. There was little dirt on my clothes from all the digging, chopping and burying, and no blood; I took special care to avoid that—but still I would've rather not had Erica scrutinizing my appearance before I had a chance to take a shower.

"Where are you going?" She said, as though I owed her explanation.

I stopped, only turning halfway toward her. "Upstairs to shower then go to bed. It's late."

"But..."

"But what, Erica?" I had thought long and hard about what I would say to her if she were here when I got back. "What?"

She hesitated. "The contract...did you meet with Michael to—"

"No. He never showed." That was the story I had decided on five minutes from pulling up to the house. There was no need to create some elaborate spider web of lies: easier to get caught in. This way was much simpler. I set foot on the first stair, grabbed the banister and was about to head up.

"But...I spoke to him. He said he was waiting for you."

"I don't know. Maybe he was waiting in the wrong place. Or maybe he decided he didn't want to go through with it after all. Could it be he didn't want to do the family thing again, like you thought he did?" I said, stepping down from the stair, walking toward my wife.

Erica looked as though she was searching her memory of his behavior to see if that was possible. "But he…"

"He what? Promised?" I said, stopping two feet in front of her. "He cheated on his wife for ten years. What's makes you think he'd do any better by you: his side piece, the mother of his bastard son." I stared into my wife's eyes, watching for any detectable flinch, any quiver of her lips or tearful blink of her eye. I knew what I said hurt her; it hurt me to say it. But she remained there, stone faced, as though she cared so little for me now that nothing I said could harm her. "You coming to bed?" I asked.

Her jaws tight, she said, "No."

"Suite yourself," I said, going for the stairs.

On the second floor I slowed as I approached David's room, but did not stop. I didn't have the nerve to go in there, see him again when I had no idea of how all this was going to play out, even though now, I knew for sure, Michael would not reclaim his place as the boy's father.

39

When I woke up the next morning, Erica wasn't lying beside me, neither was she downstairs. She had taken David with her wherever she went, but surprisingly, I wasn't concerned where that was, or if she would be returning to me, for I knew she would be; there was no longer Michael to run to.

Downstairs, wearing the clothes I had plucked from the carpet beside the bed: the clothes I had peeled off last night: the same clothes I had buried Michael in, I stood in front of the fridge drinking from a bottle of orange juice, feeling less burdened than I had at any time in the last couple of weeks. I no longer felt threatened, that I was in a competition for the best father award or that my future with my family was in jeopardy. That's not to say I believed there wasn't a chance Erica would still leave me, but I did believe it would be a lot less likely.

Shutting the fridge door, a bagel in hand, I tore a chunk out of it, and chewing, I decided I wanted to be productive on my last day off of work.

I walked through the house, opened the front door, stepped out on the porch, let the warm sun hit my face, took another bite of the bagel and stretched. That moment I couldn't help but wonder where my wife was and what she was doing: holding our son in her arms, standing in a hallway outside of some hotel room door, banging impatiently with one hand, the other holding her ringing cell phone while she waited, wondering why Michael wasn't picking up.

My cell phone vibrated in my pocket. I fished it out, answering the call.

"Pope, what's up, dude?" I said from the porch as I looked at the condition of the front lawn. It was long, needing immediate attention.

"I'm not going in till late today. Wanted to check on you. Wanna grab some breakfast at Flying Biscuit? My treat."

"Yes indeed," I said. "I'll eat anytime as long as you're buying. Why don't you scoop me in an hour? I'm gonna cut the grass real quick then shower."

After hanging up, I went to the garage, raised the rolling door and found the lawnmower pushed into a corner. I grabbed it by its handle, moved it toward the door, but thought to check the gas inside first. I unscrewed the cap on the tank, and saw that it was nearly empty. That wasn't a problem because I kept two 1-gallon refill tanks in the garage. I walked to the wall of shelves, grabbed one of the containers and was surprised to find it empty when three weeks ago, I knew I had gone to the station to have them both filled.

Shrugging it off, I figured I must've only filled one. I set the empty container aside, grabbed the other to find that it too, felt empty. I unscrewed the cap on the container to take a look inside, and yes, there was no gas. I looked left then right, casually searching the garage for anything suspicious. Hands on my hips, puzzled, I paced the dust covered floor in my slippers, considering scenarios to explain the missing gasoline, dismissing them one after another, until I stopped abruptly, turned to look back at the containers, shaking my head. "No," I said. I walked over, stopped in front of them, crossing my arms, scrutinizing every detail about them as if the cans themselves could tell me why they were no longer filled. "No," I said again to myself. "I won't believe it. I can't believe that."

I shook my head free of the disturbing thought I was entertaining, pushed the lawnmower back into the corner and closed up the garage so I could shower and get ready for breakfast with Pope.

"By the look of you, everything's working out okay," Pope said, shoveling scrambled cheese eggs into his mouth."

I sat on the other side of the booth, cutting into my seafood omelet. I was starving; I hadn't had an appetite like this in a while. "Yeah, it kinda is," I said, scooping a forkful of eggs and shrimp into my mouth.

"And that guy..." Pope said, lowering his voice and leaning forward across the table. "...who's people died in that fire. He still coming around?"

I was in mid gulp from the cup of my orange juice when Pope asked the question. I swallowed what was in my mouth, set down the cup, then said, "Nope. No longer a problem."

"What happened to him?"

I shrugged my shoulders and raised my eyebrows, appearing clueless. "He just...disappeared."

40

Erica came home a little after 8 P.M. that same day. I was sunken into the sofa cushions, watching some movie on HBO. To my surprise, she set David down on the sofa next to me. The boy crawled into my lap, playfully slapped my face a few times then jumped on my thighs as though it were the floor of a bouncy house.

"I'm cooking tacos for dinner. That okay?" Erica said, sounding neither resentful nor thrilled about it.

"Sure," I said, trying to mask the surprise in my voice. She leaned over the back of the sofa, lightly kissed my cheek, which surprised me even more.

"Be done in half an hour."

Holding the wriggling boy in my arms, I nearly broke my neck craning to watch her walk into the kitchen, wondering if someone had body-snatched my wife. Forty minutes later, Erica and I were eating while David pushed taco meat and corn nibblets into his mouth with his hands.

"Slow down over there, Lil' Man," I said, smiling at him. "Food's not going anyway."

He laughed, smearing more of the food juice onto his cheeks.

"So when you going back to work?" Erica asked, attempting to make small talk during the otherwise quiet dinner.

"Going back on Monday," I said. "Been out long enough. Really looking forward to getting back to the kids. I miss them."

"I'm sure they miss you, too," Erica said. She looked up at me a moment, then looked back down and continued chewing her food.

I didn't really know what to think of any of what was happening.

Erica had served my food, made sure everything was perfect for me, then before sitting down herself, said: "I think I'm going to have some wine. Would you like some?"

"No, thanks," I smiled, feeling almost euphoric at how things were turning out. Who needed alcohol? "I think I'm good."

"I think you really should have some with me," she insisted.

"Oh, okay. Fine," I said, not needing to be asked twice. She nodded her head, went to the cabinet, pulled down two wine glasses, opened a bottle of red, and took her time—her back to me—pouring us two healthy servings.

At the table, we held the glasses up, preparing to toast.

"To…" I asked.

"New beginnings," Erica said.

"New beginnings," I echoed.

The food was delicious, the conversation more lively than usual, but the mood felt slightly off—dreamlike: like we were on a stage set, both of us performing, reading rehearsed lines. There was no discussion of Michael. It was like he had never entered our lives, like he had never existed.

After dinner, Erica stood to remove our plates from the table.

I pulled mine toward me. "You cooked. I can clean up."

She forced a smile. "It's fine. Why don't you take David up, get him ready for bed and I'll take care of this."

I hoisted David out of his chair, carrying him out of the kitchen, but turned to Erica just before stepping out the door, David pulling on my earlobe. "Thanks," I said.

She looked back from the dishes she was loading into the dishwasher and simply said, "Sure."

"Is it over?" I asked David fifteen minutes as he smacked the surface of the sudsy bathwater with his open palms, his hair wet and thick with baby shampoo. I sat on the edge of the tub staring at the bathroom door, expecting something crazy and dramatic to happen: an explosion, the door flying off the hinges, Erica stepping through it holding an Uzi, peppering me with bullets, then pulling her dripping son out of the tub, cradling him in her arms and stepping over my bloody body to leave.

I shook the thought, chalking it up to guilt for what I did to Michael.

David's eyes were on me, a look of concern in them: as much concern as a toddler can express.

"It was justified, Lil' Guy. I swear it was."

He smiled, and continuing splashing in the tub. I dressed him in his pajamas and lay him in bed. He stared up at me with his big eyes.

"I love you," I said, mussing the soft curls on his head. "And I really think we're going to be fine."

"Wuv you too, Dawdy," David said.

217

I kissed his forehead, pulled his comforter up to under his chin, then turned off his bedroom light and left the door cracked.

Walking into my bedroom, I was surprised to see my wife there, instead of hiding out in the guest bedroom. She was standing in the center of the room, wearing a nightgown, no expression on her face, just staring forward at nothing in particular.

I stood in the doorway, not knowing what to say.

She faced me. "David go down okay?" She asked, breaking the awkward silence.

"Yeah. Fine," I smiled, stepping clumsily into the room, almost not remembering how to act with my wife in it at bedtime. "I'm...uh, guess I'm gonna take a shower." I took two steps to the bathroom, then stopped and asked: "So are you sleeping in here tonight?"

"What happened?" Erica asked, lowering herself to the edge of the bed, ignoring my question.

"What happened with what?"

"Last night...when you were supposed to meet him...to sign the contract?"

It's not as though I thought she might have forgotten about all of that, but that she might've have re-thought her expectations, realized that, all things considered, our situation was fine the way things had been, and decided to drop the fantasy of her and Michael ever being together.

"I told you. He never showed."

"I can't believe that. Why would he do that?" she asked, no malice, spite or resentment in her tone. She wasn't frowning or scowling, looking at me as though she suspected me of foul play. The words came out as a simple question she wanted to know the answer to, like asking if there would be rain tomorrow.

"I don't know what else to tell you, Erica."

"Did you do something to him?"

The bluntness of her question caught me off guard, even though I knew it should've been coming. "Wha...what are you talking about?"

She stepped right in front of me, looked me dead in the eyes. "I've called him I don't know how many times, left messages that he hasn't returned."

"Why are you telling me about this man?" I asked, getting angry. "Why are you asking me about him as though I should care whether or not—"

She spoke over me, raising her voice. "I went to the hotel where he's staying, and they said he hasn't been there...they haven't seen him in two days."

"And?" I said, raising my voice. "What are you asking me again?"

"If you did something to him?" She shouted. "Did you hurt him? Did you kill him?"

I wanted to laugh in her face, act as though I had no earthly idea of what she was talking about, act like I could never do such a thing. But she new better: I had confessed to what I was capable of when I told her about Rasul. Now I said nothing, just stood stoic before her, silent.

Her face crumpled with what seemed her realization that I had something to do with Michael's disappearance. "You did, didn't you?"

"I didn't say I did anything."

"What did you do to him? Answer me!"

I turned my back on her, but she saw my reflection in the mirror over the dresser: the guilt I could not hide was plain on my face.

"Then I'm...I'm calling the police," she said, walking toward the door to leave.

"So that we can both confess to murder?" I said.

The words stopped her, the doorknob in her hand, the door partway open.

"What happened to the gas in the cans in the garage, Erica?" I watched her in the mirror turning toward me. I did the same so that I could address her face to face.

"What are you talking about, Stan?"

"I was going to cut the grass this morning and found both cans empty, even though I know I filled them a few weeks ago."

"You're obviously mistaken," she said, appearing antsy all of sudden.

"That night, a couple of weeks ago when you got out of bed, you hadn't realized you woke me, had you? I thought you were just getting up for water or to use the bathroom, but I heard the garage door opening, went to the window to see you driving away. I thought to call you, but something told me not to. I lay back down, and when you came in, I opened my eyes just enough to check the time on the alarm clock; it was three hours later, Erica."

"You're not making any sense, Stan. When are you talking about?"

"The night your boyfriend's wife and children died." It was the only explanation I could come up with this morning for the missing gas and for her three-hour disappearance that night. I didn't want to think it: the image of my wife sneaking around the man's yard in the dark, dousing the walls of his house with gasoline, lighting it on fire, then sticking around long enough to see the flames race up to the roof, before hurrying to her car and driving home to climb back in bed with me. I couldn't believe it when the idea slithered into my head this morning, but looking at her face now, the guilt she was suffering, I knew she had done it. "What?" I said, walking over to her. "I wasn't good enough for you? Or you just wanted him back that badly that you'd kill his wife and children? What the fuck, Erica?"

She looked past me, her eyes unblinking; she didn't say a word.

"Say something!"

She jumped, startled. "I have nothing to say," she said, forcing calm into her voice.

We stood facing each other in silence for nearly a minute: me now seeing her as a murderer, as she had been seeing me since I had committed the same act. In her mind, she was probably wondering how she could be so stupid as not to stop at one of the half dozen corner gas stations she probably passed on the way back from Michael's house, before setting the cans back into the garage empty.

"Do you still need to call the police?" I asked, smugly.

"I don't see any point in that," Erica said.

"Because if you think you must, be my guest. Go right ahead."

"I said no," she said, staring me in the eyes.

"Good. Then I'm going to take a shower. I expect you to be in this bed when I come out. Okay?"

She lowered her chin, sighed and said, "Okay."

When I stepped out the bathroom, the lights were off. I heard Erica's slight movements under the comforter, and wearing just boxer shorts, I slid in bed with her. She was facing away from me, a pillow bunched under her head, I assumed, hoping I'd have nothing to say to her. From my back, I rolled up on an elbow, leaned over her shoulder. "Good night," I said, pausing there, expecting to resume the ritual from before things went south, when we'd kiss and say goodnight before going to bed.

It took longer than I liked, but hesitantly, she rolled back to face me, allowing me to softly press my lips to hers.

"Good night, Stan," she said with the tone of a criminal who had been given a lengthy sentence, but one he thought he could deal with: one he believed he could survive. She rolled back onto her side away from me. I slid up behind her. To my surprise, she did not try to stop me as I molded my body to hers, wrapped my arm around her, pressed my face into her hair and fell asleep.

41

I woke with a slight headache and little fogginess, but had an otherwise, wonderful night's sleep. Things weren't perfect between Erica and I, but the stalemate we reached put us in a position where neither could rat the other out without expecting serious consequences. And if dinner last night was any indication, things between us should be okay.

In bed, my eyes open, I didn't move, just lay there, one foot peaking out the bottom of the comforter, the top of the blanket falling to just below my navel. I turned my head. One of the pillows, obscuring part of my view, I saw that Erica was not in the king-sized bed. It didn't matter, I smiled to myself, she'd be downstairs in the kitchen, feeding our child, brewing coffee and making me breakfast as she had done before all of this nonsense started.

I had taken a life, I thought, throwing back a corner of the comforter and climbing out of bed. Some of the guilt still clung to me, making me feel I'd never completely shake it, but it was lessoning. I dragged myself toward the bathroom, my limbs feeling particularly heavy. I attributed it to too much wine. I shaved and dressed for school. Wearing khakis, shirt and a tie, I trotted down the stairs feeling a little better unburdened and hopeful about the fresh new start I knew my wife and I were about to embark upon.

I descended the last stair, smiling wider in anticipation of seeing my son, in anticipation of sitting and having coffee with my wife, talking about nothing, or talking in depth about what just happened and how we move past it.

"Erica," I called, turning the corner into the kitchen, but was immediately silenced not seeing breakfast cooking or any sign of Erica or David.

"Erica?" I called, walking through the living room, glancing out the window, noticing that her car wasn't in the driveway. I walked back through the house a little quicker than before, stopped at the door that opened into the garage, flung it back to see that her car was not there either. I slammed the door closed, started quickly toward the stairs, my pace increasing to a run by the time I had reached them. I climbed them two at a time, forcing out of my head thoughts of the frightful act I prayed she hadn't committed while I slept.

On the second floor, I ran toward our bedroom, but stopped short at David's door. I pushed it open, flipped up the light switch on the wall, and frantically scanned the room. It looked normal: blankets on the bed twisted as they always were when he had slept there. His stuffed animals were untouched all around the room, the storybooks I'd read to him at night were stacked by his nightstand.

I went to his dresser, yanked out the top drawers. They slid out with little resistance for they were empty. I gasped, yanking on the second row, then the third. All six drawers were as bare as when the dresser was new. I went to his closet and there were a few items still there hanging from the rack, but more than half his clothes were gone.

"No!" I said, running back to my bedroom. "No, Erica!"

Inside, I did as I had done in my son's room: yanked all the drawers, threw open the closet door. Most of Erica's clothes were gone, as well as her two large suitcases and her weekend bag. She'd taken all her belongings and all of my son's into the guest bedroom in preparation to move it, but she's hasn't done that yet, I told myself, as I ran out and threw open the door of the guest bedroom. Breathing heavily, holding onto the knob, I was saddened at what I saw: a completely clean room, not a sign of disarray: no toddler's shirt on the floor, no woman's pump laying on its side by bathroom door; the room was cleaned out. I asked myself how could she have done all that without waking me? When could she have had the time? Then I caught sight of the red fluorescent numbers on the bedside alarm clock. It wasn't 7 in the morning, as I had thought, but 12:15 in the afternoon.

Immediately I thought back to last night at dinner: her insistence that I drink with her: how long it took her to poor my initial glass of wine. Had my wife slipped me something to make me sleep, knowing that early this morning, she'd be leaving me?

I walked into the room, my head hung, noticing the bed was perfectly made, and on top of it, a single sheet of white printer paper, lines of scribbled sentences crowding both sides of the page. I lowered myself onto the bed, not looking at the letter behind me, hoping it'd disappear if I chose not to acknowledge it.

"Please, don't have taken my son," I said under my breath over and over again, rocking gently on the bed, my eyes closed. "Please, don't have taken my son. Please, don't have taken my son."

I turned around, and like ripping the bandage from a tender wound, I quickly grabbed the letter and forced myself to look at it. It was not addressed to me; there was no opening. Her words just started at the top of the page.

Years ago when Michael told me he'd never leave his wife for me, I started looking for someone like you. When I found you, I told myself you'd be enough to keep my mind off him. But when he wanted to see me, I jumped at the chance. I got pregnant with David because I lied to him, told him I was on birth control and I couldn't get pregnant. I told him it was okay to come in me. It was what I needed: to feel his warm fluid spill into me. He gave me the child I always wanted from him. I thought when I told him about it in front of you, offered to allow you to father his child, he would've surely forbidden it. I thought he would've left his family. I thought he would want to be with me and raise his baby. When he wasn't as happy as I was, and agreed to give his child away, that hurt me more than you could ever know. Once David was born, I wanted to take him to Michael's house, show his bitch of a wife who her husband really was and force their marriage to end. But there was you. What would you have thought to see me act that way? You loved me, wanted nothing more than to raise David with me, when Michael abandoned him. All I could do was accept you, even though I still wanted him.

You grew to love David like he was your own, even though he never could be and never will be. For that, I think I owe you an apology. It will be the one and only one you'll get. I'm sorry for making you believe that the three of us could ever be happy together forever.

Truth is, I had never stopped loving Michael, and I had never stopped seeing him. Even the night after he signed our baby over to you, I told you I had to work late so that I could go make love to him. He was the reason you and I had sex so seldom after David was born: all my needs were being met by him.

The older David got, the more I needed to see him with his natural father: the more I wanted to be with the man that gave me my son. I asked him constantly to leave his wife. I begged him to, but he always told me no. After giving him a son and twelve years of devotion, I just could not accept that for an answer again.

Michael had no knowledge of what I was planning, but I took matters into my own hands, knowing I could give him no other choice but me. And just like I thought, after his wife and children were removed, he wanted me and his son back. But you took the man I loved away from me. As you probably guessed, I drugged you last night, and so I'm taking the son you love away from you.

I know how much you love David. I hope you sitting there reading this letter is tearing a hole so big in your heart it will never close. That's how I feel.

We're even Stan: in the beautiful people we've lost and the horrible things we've done to try to hold onto them. We're even. So I'm leaving you and I'm taking my son. It's best you forget David. Do not try to find us. If you do, I'll tell the police all I know about what you've done. I might not have evidence, but you did kill two people. I'm sure if they dig around enough, they'll find something to land you in prison for the rest of your life. And for what I've done: it's something I'll just have to live with.

Goodbye.

42

I had sat on the edge of that bed crying, that letter crinkled in my fist, for an hour. Afterward, I smeared the tears from my face, stood, walked into my bedroom, grabbed my suitcase from the closet, lay it open on the bed I shared with my wife, and started to throw clothes into it.

An hour later, I stood at Serena's door, holding that suitcase in my hand, waiting for someone to answer the door. I heard movement, felt the pressure of footsteps approaching making me nervous: made me question if I still had a place here, or if I'd be turned away.

If I was, where would I go? Who would love me like I loved David, like I loved Erica?

The door opened.

"Dad?" Janis said, standing in front of me, wearing fraying jeans, and faded tee from the university she used to attend. I didn't respond to her, just stared at her in a way that must've made her feel sorry for me. She looked at the luggage in my right hand. "Dad, what are you doing here?"

"Janis, who's at the door?" I heard Serena call from somewhere deep in the house.

"I want to come home," I said to my daughter, my voice uncertain and a little shaky. "Would you be okay with that?"

My daughter's face lit up, and she threw herself into me with enough force to almost knock me over. She squeezed me tight, her face buried in my shoulder: "Yeah, yeah, Daddy. Of course!" She pulled away from me, smiling, after kissing my cheek.

"That's what you say, but do you think your mother—"

"Janis, what's—" Serena said, seeing me and her daughter standing in the front doorway.

"Dad wants to ask you something, Mom," Janis said, squeezing my hand, standing fidgety and jittery beside me with excitement.

Serena had already seen the suitcase that had fallen to my feet—and probably as her daughter had—already read the wounded expression on my face and figured why I was there. Tears already clouding my eyes, a lump the size of an apple was growing in my throat. "I know you said if I didn't take the opportunity you were giving me the other day, I'd never be given another one, but do you think—"

Before I could finish speaking, Serena had come to me, wrapped her arms around my neck as my daughter had. "I'm sorry things went the way they did," she whispered in my ear, no doubt understanding that was the reason I had returned. Being Serena, she was cool enough to accept me back regardless, and said, "You know this will always be your home."

"Are you sure?" I asked.

She looked me in the eyes and was about to speak when—

"She's sure," Janis said for her, interrupting. "You're my Dad." Janis wrapped one arm around my shoulder, the other around her mother's. "We're a family, how could Mom not be sure."

"That simple, huh?" I asked my daughter.

"It's always been that simple," she said, glancing at each of us. "You guys just didn't know it."

END   5/31/15

Haven't heard? Read the book that came before MY WIFE'S LOVER.

Order MY WIFE'S BABY

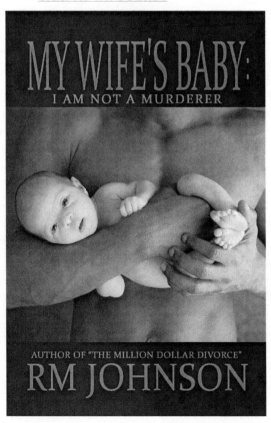

Want more RM Johnson?

Read the excerpt below from his recent novel:

HATE THE AIR: The Abbreviated Life of Shea Kennedy

Excerpt: Chapter 1

Coming out of my thoughts, I was doing sixty miles an hour down Sycamore Avenue. I noticed the door of a house swinging open, when yesterday it was closed. I squeezed the handbrake on the old Harley Davidson, whipped a U-turn, steered the bike into the driveway of the two-story house and climbed off.

The grass outside had grown knee high thick with weeds and spotted with trash. Visible just behind the glass windows of the house were iron bars and heavy drapes.

The sky overhead was dreary and full of clouds. I stood in the center of the driveway, looking up and down the street. It was deathly quiet around me: no sound of traffic, lawnmowers running, or kids screaming as they played, like before the air turned. I pushed my goggles up, readjusting the bandana—the attempt most of us made to protect ourselves from the air—over my nose and mouth.

"What do you think, boy?" I said still looking up at the house.

The question was for my partner, Tornado, a five year-old German Shepard: ninety pounds of muscle, he wore a vest and harness from his Police dog days. He was dark brown with a black saddle, paws, muzzle, and superhero mask of dark fur around his eyes. He had a splash of white in the center of his breast: an inverted triangle that I thought, at ten years old, looked like a tornado.

I checked his tether to the sidecar. "Make sure no one makes off with our wheels, okay boy." He licked my hand and whined as I started cautiously up the walkway and climbed the stairs. I stuck my head inside the house. "Anyone in there?" I could barely see anything for the thick, dark curtains pulled over all the windows; it was nearly pitch black inside. I told myself not to slip, not get jumped, get caught of guard and killed. The possibility now was always in the back of my head.

I eased the Walther handgun my father gave me from my shoulder holster, pulled my flashlight and clicked it on, pointing them both at the space in front of me. It was something he had taught me, knowing how much I wanted to follow his path—to be like him.

One morning years ago while Dad was getting ready for work, I pushed open the bedroom door, slipped into his room, hoping to catch him polishing his shoes for work, but instead, saw his gun belt hanging from the bedroom chair. I slid the weapon from its holster, held it with both hands toward the bathroom door. When Dad stepped out in his uniform trousers and undershirt, I tried to pull the trigger, but was not strong enough.

"Pow! You're dead, Daddy!" I said, wondering why he didn't smile, fall to the floor, splay his arms and legs, laughing. He rushed me, snatched the gun, and wrangled me to him as though saving me from a burning building.

I had gotten the "Don't-you-ever-touch-this-again!" lecture, followed by the "Don't-you-know-how-dangerous-guns-are!" speech.

Sitting on his lap, I watched him eject the wheel of the revolver and empty the bullets from the gun.

"We can't ever let your mother know this happened, understand?" Dad said, holding me around the waist on his lap. "She'd have both of us locked up." He paused, looked up as though figuring something. "If you're really that interested in guns, you should learn the proper way to use them."

"You'll teach me?" I asked, excited.

"How old are you again?" he said, like he didn't know.

"Nine." I said, hoping that was old enough for whatever he planned to teach me.

A week later, sun shinning dimly through the dark green skins of a half dozen beer bottles Dad had carefully stacked on our fence, he watched as I focused my attention over the site of a handgun, my finger locked around the trigger.

Over the previous week, he had taught me how to hold and aim, how to holster, dismantle, clean a gun and put it together again. I picked that stuff up fast. But as I stood in the yard trying to shoot the weapon, it felt as though the trigger hadn't moved in years; it wouldn't budge.

"Fire the weapon, Shea! Do you need me to show you how again?" Dad called from across the yard.

"No Dad!" I said, determined not to fail him.

One eye closed, looking again down the site at the green bottle furthest to the left, I pulled back the trigger, squeezing until I felt the little metal sliver would slice through my finger. The gun popped, kicked in my hands, staggering me back two steps in the mud. At the same time the bottle shattered with a high-pitched tinkle in the distance. I smiled turning to Dad, hearing him laughing, seeing him running toward me, his arms raised.

"You did it!" He grabbed me up, twirled me in circles. I was happy. What I had done made him proud, and I wanted him to be proud of me like that everyday for the rest of my life. So every evening at dusk, the sun dropping behind the high trees, I stood in our huge one-acre backyard, in that muddy or dusty patch—depending on the weather—knocking off bottles from the fence.

After three months I had gotten to the point where I'd become a crack shot. That's what Dad started calling me—a "crack shot!"

At not yet 10 years old, I could snatch the gun from the old leather holster, and in seconds, get a bead on those bottles, slicing them all in half. I'd stand there, gun held out before me smoking after shattering six bottles, sparing not a single bullet.

No more cheers from Dad after my displays of marksmanship, he'd stand in awe then slowly walk to me, chest held out, prideful.

"If anything ever happens to me, I know you'll be fine," Dad said on one of those days, hugging me. My face pressed to the belly of his red and black flannel shirt, I wondered what he meant by that. Nothing would ever happen to Dad. It would've been hard for anyone to convince me that he would ever die: but impossible to prove that when he did, I would be to blame.

I stepped into the open door of the house. I saw no signs of a break-in: the living room hadn't been ransacked: no furniture upended, cushions knifed open, legs torn off end tables, or lamps broken like cracked egg shells on the carpet. It was the opposite: books lay neatly on the coffee table, burned down candles sat beside them, pocket change: pennies, dimes and a quarter were spread nearby. The kitchen was clean: no trash overflowing in the corner pail. But the cabinet doors hung open. Inside of them there was nothing.

I climbed the stairs, stopped in the second floor hallway, surrounded by four doors, all of them closed. I reached to open one, heard movement behind another, spun and with a grunt, kicked it open. The shadow of a boy rummaging through drawers whirled around, and in the splash of flashlight, I saw the gun as it was turned on me.

"Don't do it. I'll shoot!" I cried, my voice tense, high pitched, terrified. The
flashlight beam bounced around his body and face, the thing trembling uncontrollable in my hand. He wore dark pants, a sweater and a ski mask pulled over his head.

"Whatever you have, put it down now!" I demanded.

"Who are you?"

"Sheriff!" I said, trying to sound authoritative.

"Legacy?" He scoffed.

"Freakin sheriff!" I said, again, jabbing my gun at him. "Put it down now or I'll—" before I could finish, I felt an excruciating pain shoot through my skull, shudder down my spine, dropping me to the floor. Movement around me, I felt someone step over me, wrench my gun from my hand. My flashlight lay somewhere on the floor, casting a tall, oblong, light circle in the corner of the room. Within it stood the stretched shadow of the boy who had knocked me over the head from behind. He grinned, pulled his bandana down, revealing yellow crooked teeth.

"You about to say you was gonna shoot my friend?" The boy asked, pressing the side of his gun to my head.

I raised my palms, expecting to die, and thinking how disappointed Dad would've been if he could see me now. "Please," I begged.

"It's a little late for that," he said, grinning wider, dragging the tip of the gun down my face, pressing it against my cheek so hard I cried out.

"Stop!" The boy I had snuck up on, said. "We're not here to kill. Food is all we need. Besides, she's the sheriff."

The boy with the ugly grin looked harder at me. A glint of flashlight caught the point of a star on my badge. He reached down to snatch it. I grabbed his hand before he could tear it off of me, fought him for it, was ready to die before I let him take it.

"Leave it!" the boy wearing the black mask ordered.

He came up behind Yellow Grin, yanked him off of me, pointed his gun at me, while holding out his palm to his partner, gesturing for him to hand over my gun. He ejected the magazine, the bullet in the chamber and pushed both into his pocket, then threw my gun across the room. He handed the bag of stolen goods to his creepy friend and told him to take it outside.

I stared at the boy through the eyeholes in his mask, watching him, wondering if he'd kill me.

"Mother or father was a cop? Probably your hero, and you're trying to do what they did," he said, his gun still on me. "Right?"

My heart pounding, I couldn't speak, could barely breath.

"Things are different. No more heroes. Just people gagging in the street, and people who *gonna* gag in the street. Leave this place like everybody else, before you get yourself killed."

He shoved his gun in the waist of his pants, turned, left me on the floor, shaking, terrified of moving until I heard the downstairs door slam shut. I rolled on my belly, shimmied across the carpet, grabbed my flashlight then found my gun.

Downstairs, I stepped out on the porch, shielded my eyes against the piercing sunlight. Tornado barked frantically at me as though he knew I had acted stupidly—almost got myself killed trying to defend an empty house.

"Shhh, boy. Shhh!" I told him.

I climbed on my bike, kick-started the engine, about to pull off, when the realization that I had almost died hit me hard. Tears came to my eyes and with both gloved fists, I started hitting the bike's dented gas tank, screaming as Tornado barked louder. "Why would you leave me with this? Why would you think I could do it? Why, Dad?" I cried.

I hammered the tank over and over until my hands ached, finally lowering them on the dented metal. I stayed like that, stretched over the bike until I could stop crying.

Tornado had gone silent, too. I looked at him. He stared back, his head tilted to a side as if to say, now that you got that out of your system, can we please go?

I smiled a little, wiped my face and sat up straight on the bike. Glancing upward, I said, "Sorry Dad, for acting like a little girl. Won't happen again, okay."

I pulled down my goggles, toed the Harley into gear then sped off.

RM Johnson is the award-winning author of twenty novels. They include the bestselling Harris Men series, The Million Dollar and The Keeping the Secret series. He holds an MFA in Creative Writing and currently resides, happily, in Atlanta, Georgia.

Find more titles from RM Johnson

RM Johnson would love to hear your comments.
Email RM at **RMnovels@yahoo.com**
Friend him at **Facebook.com/RMNovels**

CPSIA information can be obtained
at www.ICGtesting.com
Printed in the USA
LVOW12s2133240717

542441LV00003B/787/P